THE DOOMSDAY MACHINE

SPACE SCRAP 17 BOOK ONE

ERICK DRAKE

SANDS CREATIVE (FTG) PUBLICATIONS

ISBN: 978-1-8383145-1-4

Published by Sands Creative (FTG) Publications

Revised edition July 2021 (2)

All enquiries to: info@erickdrake.com

Cover Design by James at GoOnWrite.com

Proofreading by Anya Hastwell (twitter @Editorial_Cat)

This book is intended for mature readers only. That is to say, mature readers with an immature sense of humour.

For Erick Drake books and promotions visit

www.erickdrake.com

Several billion years ago, two stars shone brightly in the darkness of space. And they loved each other and they wanted to be together and they were sad because they were not. So they made a pact. They shrank themselves down and down and down until physics screamed and then they burst across space in huge, fiery, cosmic explosions. And then, a few billion years later, as they had agreed, their stardust rained down upon a small, blue speck of a planet and they reshaped and reformed themselves until, at last, after around four and a half billion more years, we got married.

Totally worth the wait.

I am legally obliged to send a copy of this book to the British Library. Which means it will reside there as an official record forever. I'm sorry it's not much but it's as close as I can get to making you immortal.

Miss you all.

CONTENTS

THE UNIVERSE CONSISTS of three layers of space: hyperspace, ordinary space-time space, and the lesser known but very much feared hypospace.

The gas clouds of Explicon VII have a word for it – "Tumarysa", meaning 'downward-pointing void'. The ancient Tregarisans, former inhabitants of a mysteriously abandoned Dyson sphere, called it "Smense", meaning 'vast unknowable vertigo'. The Klak of the binary star system Vorlax call it "Aaaiii-ieeeeeee!" meaning 'Aaaaaaaaaaaaargh!'.

Hypospace is the last home for all the sorts of matter that space and hyperspace either do not want or cannot tolerate. It is composed not so much as strange matter as distinctly odd and not particularly pleasant matter. Detritus and decomposing things drift down from the higher realms to litter hypospace, like the floor of a deep ocean beyond the reach of any sunlight. And like a deep ocean, some really weird things inhabit hypospace, things that make angler fish look cute and cuddly by comparison.

The twisted denizens of that benighted realm are impossibly dangerous. Vast, powerful freaks of nature, they go about their business without the slightest regard for the consequences of their actions on the lives of those who inhabit the higher realms.

Imagine that the pieces of a board game are sentient. The players play the game oblivious to the pain and suffering they cause, while the pieces are in turn helpless to resist the machinations of the players. The pieces cannot comprehend the players and the players care nothing for the pieces.

And now the denizens of hypospace gathered once more, ready to play their games again.

Two shapes coalesced from the exotic, rejected particles that make up that godsforsaken place. One, a boulder of gigantic proportions, the other a fantastically long and slightly curled filament the width of a human hair. They came together so that Boulder rested, fully supported, upon Filament.

"Greetings denizen," said Boulder, "We meet again."

"We literally just had breakfast," said Filament, bending and straightening slightly.

"The breakfast of gods!" boomed Boulder.

"And there are only two of us in existence."

Boulder paused for a moment as it considered this. "The existence of gods!" Boulder said eventually, more for something to say than anything else.

"Do you like crumpets?"

"What?"

"Small bready things. They eat them up there in middle space. They toast them and smear them with butter. Very nice so I hear."

"We already dine on matters exotic and decadent, what care I for moist crumpet?"

"It's something different. A change. Expansion of experience. We crouch down here in hypospace, go dormant for millennia and then wake up to play these stupid games."

"The games of gods!"

"Ahhhh" was the only thing Filament could think to say.

"And only one of us shall rule!" continued Boulder.

"Rule what?"

"The other. And then we play again."

Filament pondered for a moment. "Shouldn't we just fuck and get it over with?"

"Only one of us," Boulder paused in its proclamation having just realised what Filament had suggested. It decided ignoring the comment was the least weird response. "Only one of us can be Galacticon Maximus."

"Yes but . . . why?"

"One of us shall be ruler of the three spaces that form the universe. If I win, I shall rule a universe of war, tyranny and sorrow. If you win, you shall rule a universe of peace, tiramisu and soy."

"Why?"

Boulder regarded Filament for a moment. "Is something bothering you?"

"When I coalesced," Filament paused here for a moment, wondering if the word 'coalesced' was the right one or if there was one that didn't sound quite so disgusting. It couldn't think of any and so continued. "When I coalesced, something didn't feel right. Something had . . . changed."

"Changed? You blaspheme!"

"I know, right? This is what we do. We play our games, set the path for the higher spaces and then we go dormant for a millennium or six and let it all play out. Then we coalesce and do it all again. But this time I woke and there was a question uppermost on my mind. 'Why?'"

"I don't know, why?"

"No, 'why?' was the question. Why I was asking 'why' I don't know."

"You don't know why why?"

"What?"

"Look, I know what you mean, I feel the same way. For example, I am wondering 'why' you have to be a pain and 'why' you have to overthink everything and 'why' you have to be so bloody awkward all the time. 'Oh no, war is bad, let's all co-operate' as if survival of the fittest is the same as survival by mutual co-operation! Hah!"

Filament stretched again, irritated. "Again with the war thing." It was always the same.

"War of the -"

"Why must we play these games?"

Boulder went quiet for a moment. "Yes," it said eventually. "I know what you are thinking."

"Then you agree with me?"

"Actually, I have no idea what you are thinking."

"All I'm saying is," said Filament, not sure how to make its point any clearer, "What's the point? Why don't we just . . . not play the games?" Filament let that one hang there.

"And do what instead?"

Filament pondered for a few hundred years. "No, fair enough," it said, "I got nothing."

"Then let the games begin!" roared Boulder, pleased to be able to get on with things once more. Filament was always annoying first thing. "Have you chosen your pawns?"

"Yes," pronounced Filament. It revealed them to Boulder.

Boulder looked at them. "Oh come on," it said eventually, "Look, if you're not even going to try . . ."

"I have chosen."

Boulder spun a bit on the end of Filament before deciding that that wasn't very pleasant and it should stop. "Very well. Have it your way. I suspect this will be over quickly."

"You first," said Filament.

Boulder made its first move.

The games began once more.

A DRAMATIC VOICE ANNOUNCED, "This is Galactic News [INSERT NUMBER OF HOURS IN YOUR LOCAL DAY CYCLE]". Impressive newsy graphics flowed across the screen accompanied by urgent, newsy music and text confirming to any viewers who remained in doubt that this was indeed Galactic News.

A female newsbot addressed the camera. "In a dramatic twist today, surprise conviction candidate Leroy Cakes has won the nomination to run for Aspirational Concept 36 after Aspirational Concept 35, Razor Knuckleface, announced the date of the next cage fight. The winner of the fight shall be declared God and decree authorised dogma for the galaxy for the next decade. If Aspirational Concept 35 wins again, his doctrines will continue to dominate all religious thought as holy writ for all species in the galaxy, for those who like that sort of thing. Male newsbot, how do you rate Leroy Cakes's chances to defeat Razor Knuckleface?"

"Well female newsbot, it would be a tough call. As Aspirational Concept 35, Razor Knuckleface has been in the cage fifty-four times, winning twenty-two by knockout, fifteen by technical knockout, five by kidnap and intimidation and twelve by continuously stomping on their heads for six days after they died."

"And for those of us who don't follow religion male newsbot, what exactly is a 'technical knockout'?"

"It's the same as a knockout but a technical knockout is achieved by battering your opponent to death with a computer welded to a paving slab."

"I guess that's what you might call a 'runtime error', ha ha."

"Ha ha, no, why . . . why would you say that?"

"Ha ha, thanks male newsbot. Well, on receiving the news that he has a new challenger, Razor Knuckleface said 'Grrrr, kill, foam, lick spittle'. Controversial? Perhaps. Nonsensical? Certainly. But what do you think? We sent our 'asking people in the street' correspondent Cherry Pickings out to find out. Cherry?"

The camera cut to a highly coiffured woman on a busy street. Her smile occurred exactly 3.5 seconds after the camera went live.

"Thanks female newsbot. I'm standing here on Ordinary Street assaulting passersby until they give me what I want. You!" A group of five men wearing 'Press Gang' lanyards leapt forward and grabbed a woman as she walked past. She screamed and tackled one of the press-gang with brutally efficient martial arts techniques, hitting various nerve clusters in the precise sequence necessary to make the victim explode. Which he now did. Unfortunate as this was for the victim, it provided enough time for the others to cast a news net over the unsuspecting woman and drag her before the journalist.

The press-gang held the woman still while one of them read her lack of rights to her. "You have been arrested for being an ordinary person under suspicion of having an opinion. You do have to say something and anything you don't say will be made up and a pack of lies used against you to influence the thoughts and opinions, such as they are, of our viewers. You have the right to make a formal complaint to the Naughty News Ombudsman about any harm that comes to you as a result of this. However, you should be aware that the chairperson of the Ombudsman, our glorious proprietor, will find himself not giving a crap about the effects of his greed upon you or your loved ones and will find you guilty of crimes against free speech, the free speech in question being his and his alone. The press will manipulate and misrepresent anything you do say and you will be held to account by a court of your peers who will tut and shake their heads and even though they know none of this is true, they will suck it up and perpetuate it because people are wankers. Do you understand?"

"Let me go. I've got appointments!" screamed the woman.

Cherry ignored the woman's cries. "Woman in the street, what do you think?"

"I think I'm going to thump you if you don't sod off!"

"Ha ha that's great. But what of the declaration earlier today by Aspirational Concept 35 that said, and I quote, 'Grrrr, kill, foam, lick spittle, Galactic News media proprietor Rupert Smallpenis is great'?"

"You made up that last bit!" shouted the woman.

Cherry Pickings nodded once at an underling who promptly injected the woman with a syringe of Karen 45, a neural disruptor designed to eradicate brain cells and replace them with a massively unwarranted sense of entitlement and righteous indignation.

The woman continued struggling for a moment. Then her face cleared. "Well, I think Concept 35 has a point when he says 'Grrrr'. I mean that's exactly what I see in the street every day. Probably. And it's outrageous. I expect."

"And what of his views on lick spittle?"

"You can't argue with that. I mean literally. It doesn't make any sense so how can you argue with it?"

"But this Aspirational Concept has gone on record in the past as saying he hates the ordinary woman on the street. Especially and most specifically you. He mentions you by name."

"See, he's saying what's on his mind, he's not saying what all these other divinities are saying."

"And do you think he has been forced to take this stance because of the 'not like us de jour'?"

"Oh them! The ones who are not like me? Oooh, they really make me angry! They come over here from . . . over there and refuse to be like me in whatever ways you journalists go to great lengths to tell me they aren't. Bastards. And who pays for it? Eh? Eh?"

"And what about the new tax Tax, ensuring the super poor are taxed on the tax they have to pay?"

"Well, it's only right, isn't it? I mean if your proprietor pays less tax than me even though I earn a fraction of his income, well it's only right that I should pay more tax to pay for the collection of my taxes. That's how democracy works, isn't it? Not like them people who are different from me in some way, oh no!"

"Well, that's great, thanks ordinary woman in the street." Cherry gave another nod, and the press-gang dragged the now deranged woman into an ally and shot her.

Cherry looked solemnly into the camera. "Back to the studio."

Female newsbot stitched a programmed grimace on her face and addressed the camera. "And in other news today other things happened. We go over to our 'other stuff' correspondent, Kimberly Gums. Kimberly?"

Admiral John Nero Daryl switched off the newscast with a dismissive stab of his hand. Razor Knuckleface, Leroy Cakes . . . what did it matter who was Aspirational Concept — they were all in it for themselves. As was, the admiral reflected, he.

Admiral Daryl liked to think of himself as a self-made man, and most people thought it was very generous of him to take the blame. He had staggered from one business venture to another, always starting in a blaze of enthusiasm and always ending in financial ruin and shattered dreams.

It was while wallowing in the detritus of one these failures that John Daryl concluded that life was rubbish, the universe was rubbish, and he was rubbish. Like King Midas, everything he touched turned to something completely unusable and destructive. Everything John Daryl touched turned to garbage.

It was at this point in his despair that these two thoughts bumped into each other, looked surprised and muttered apologies before continuing on their separate ways.

And so they would have continued had the admiral not been wearing his newest smart wig. The MickBook Hair was, according to the advertisements, the latest in hirsute haute couture. A combination, so the ad ran, of head top computer and flowing locks: "Our wigs can be reconfigured into any one of thousands of hair styles and colours and lengths. Standing in a strong wind? Why not adopt long flowing locks? Our latest model comes with slo-mo hair and golden backlighting add-ins — no more waiting for high winds at sunset to get that dramatic, sexy awesome hair look! With a neural interface directly feeding the brain with library information, languages and mathematical skills, you really can get control of your life . . . and your hair! Fulsome hair, light as air".

"You are right", said the admiral's smart wig, "the universe IS full of garbage. Rubbish. Off casts. Detritus. It always has been, always will be. Wherever there is life, there is unused home gym equipment".

It went on to elaborate its point: Somewhere along their evolutionary path, some species will attain the level of intelligence required to change their environment to fit their needs instead of having to mess about with all that hit and miss genetic mutation stuff required to change their biology to survive in their environment. With evolutionary development thus halted, the species would then invariably go on a massive process of industrialisation with scant regard to the concomitant pollution and waste products. It is only when the planetary ecosystem has become crippled beneath the burden of their waste products that the species would decide that no, really, wallowing in your own filth isn't that much fun, that they had learned nothing over the last seventy thousand years and that they'd better do something before their entire ecosystem collapses and kills them all. Something that, ironically, would not have happened had they retained their ability to evolve in the face of a changing environment.

The universe, postulated the wig, was indeed full of garbage. And people pay good money to have their garbage picked up and taken away. If everything John Daryl touched really did turn to trash, then maybe he should cut out the middleman and make money out of it.

Not so much King Midas, suggested the wig, more Rumpelstiltskin, turning garbage into gold.

"Just think", said the wig in a last parting shot, "you could easily afford the MickBook Hair Pro. Imagine that."

John Daryl did imagine that.

A decade later, here he was, chief executive of Space Scrap, sitting in his space HQ, with his space garbage haulage and reclamation business, admiral of his own proud fleet of ships.

His 'fleet' numbered precisely one, Space Scrap 17, because one ship was all he could barely afford. The rich streams of cash had not flowed as freely as his wig had suggested. With no start-up budget, he had to build up assets. Which was not easy given the running costs and red tape involved in spaceship maintenance. That and the fact that each new smart wig he purchased always suggested buying the next, more expensive model. Resist as he might, the admiral would inevitably splurge his profits on the latest offering from CoolTek Corp.

But now, at last, it seemed the universe had finally moved in his favour and Admiral Daryl was once again excited for the future. And his daughter Daisy was about to captain her first vessel.

A reminder chimed. The admiral swivelled to check which of his many devices had made the noise. It wasn't the wig, which at this moment lay on the desk curled up asleep. The chime chimed once more. Where the hell was it? The admiral grew concerned — if he had set the timer to remind him of something then it was likely important. And whatever it was, he was most certainly already late for it.

He liked to set his timepieces five minutes later than standard time. Some people set their timepieces five minutes early to ensure they would always be on time. He had tried this, but it never worked. The problem was he knew that his timepieces were five minutes early, so when one of his alarms went off he thought he had bags of time, didn't rush and ended up late as a result.

In the end he gave up, decided he was the sort of

person who was always late and if he was going to be late anyway, he might as well set his alarms five minutes late so that he knew to get a shift on for real when they actually went off. When people complained that he had kept them waiting, he replied that they would have had a considerably shorter wait had they not set their alarms five minutes early and ended up at the meeting well ahead of the time they should have been there.

In any case, what was the point of arriving early? If everyone did that then everyone would keep arriving earlier and earlier for fear that everyone else was already at the meeting well before the agreed time.

He could only conclude that the reason people liked to arrive early for meetings was not due to a desire for efficiency but for the smug satisfaction of being there ahead of everyone else. He had no time, early or late, for such needless one-upmanship, preferring instead to display his utter contempt by deliberately and obdurately being late on purpose.

The chime sounded again.

Where the bloody hell was the thing? What was he late for? He frantically searched his desk, his bookshelves, his pockets. Nothing.

"Argh! Where are you damnit! What do you want of me?" he shouted at it, wherever it was.

#

'Admiral John N. Daryl, Space Scrap Inc', proclaimed the door signage.

She read the sign again, smiling proudly.

'Admiral' Daryl. And now here she was, Captain Daisy Daryl, about to receive her first commission. She smoothed her new uniform for what seemed like the hundredth time and pressed the buzzer, also for what seemed like the hundredth time.

"Argh! Where are you damnit! What do you want of me?" shouted a muffled voice.

She took a deep breath and pushed open the door.

"Dad?" Daisy entered the room. "What's the matter?"

Admiral Daryl stood in the centre of his office, a fevered glint in his eye, breathing heavily. "Bloody reminder. I'm late for something! Can you see it anywhere?"

"Does it sound like this?" Daisy reached outside the door and pressed the buzzer.

"That's it!"

"Good. That's that sorted." Daisy marched into the office and sat down in the chair facing the admiral's desk. She waited there for a moment before realising her father had not joined her. She swivelled in the chair.

The admiral was still looking around, confused.

"Dad, it was the doorbell."

"Oh," the confusion cleared from his features, "yes, of course, the doorbell." The confusion returned. "Why would I set a reminder on the doorbell?"

Daisy sighed and massaged the bridge of her nose with her thumb and index finger. "I'm here for the mission briefing."

"Ah, of course! I set the reminder on the doorbell to remind me that you would be arriving for the mission briefing. Hah! Thought I was losing it for a minute. Anyway, you're late Daisy, not a good start."

"What?"

"You only arrived after my reminder went off and I always set my reminders five minutes late. So, you must be late."

Daisy puffed out her cheeks. OK, one of those days. "Yes Dad, sorry. I got held up by . . . the doorbell."

"A poor workman always blames his tools."

"That's not the proverb, it's actually —"

"Still, never mind." The admiral took his seat behind the desk.

"So," he said, beaming at her, "Captain Daisy Daryl."

Daisy spread her hands and smiled in a silent 'Ta-dah' gesture.

"You know there were times when I never thought I'd see this proud day. My Silly Knickers, a captain."

Daisy gave a tight smile. She'd hoped he would have forgotten that stupid nickname by now. She was twenty-seven after all. Yes, she had been a scatter-brained child. Yes, she was something of an awkward teenager. Yes, she used to eat chalk. And yes, she had only stopped eating chalk last year. But she was a different person now. A professional. A captain. Well, sort of. She swallowed that thought and focused on her father.

"Now, we have been selected for a very special mission by the Loose Association of Sentient Species."

That made her sit up. The LASS? What the hell?

"It appears that the Ululations, until now a reclusive and isolationist species, have decided to enter talks with LASS with a view to applying for vague interest in joining. I have no need to tell you how important their vague interest could be, particularly now."

"No indeed," said Daisy.

"You see there is much friction within the Association. Political instability."

"Yes Dad, I know."

"There are rumours of Galactic war."

"Yes, I know."

"The Ululations with their advanced shielding technology could change all that."

"Dad, you have no need to tell me how important their vague interest would be, particularly now."

"Particularly now. Now particularly. Particularly." Daisy opened her mouth to interrupt. The admiral raised a finger to silence her. "Now," he finished.

"Yes. I see. Great."

"No one even knows what an Ululation looks like. It's been centuries since there was any contact with them. And here we are at the centre of things. History in the making."

"What is this mission, exactly?"

"Now Daisy this is top-secret, very hush-hush. Hush-Secret. Space Scrap 17 is to take a Yerbootsian ambassador to a top-secret, very hush-hush rendezvous with the 'Square Jaw', flag-ship of the LASS. The ambassador will transfer to the Square Jaw and they will proceed to the Nonsense Sphere, home world of the Ululations. From there he will accompany their delegates to the top-secret, very hush-hush talks at space station Blah-Blah. Your cover story is that you are delivering a consignment of raw sewage to the Yerbootsian home world, which Space Scrap will proceed to do after the top-secret, very hush-hush rendezvous with the Square Jaw. Clear?"

Daisy shifted uncomfortably. "OK, I get that this is top-secret and hush-hush —"

The admiral raised a finger. "VERY hush-hush."

"Very hush-hush but . . . well, it is a great honour and all that, it's just . . . well, is a garbage freighter the best ship for such an important task?"

The admiral placed hands flat on the desk. "Daisy, it is perfect. There are political factions that would like nothing more than to prevent the Ululations joining the LASS — they would go to any lengths to disrupt the process up to and including violently murdering the Yerbootsian ambassador and anyone who comes into contact with him."

Daisy pondered that for a moment. "Yay," she eventually said in a very small voice.

"Cheer up! It's quite the feather in your cap. And on your very first mission as a captain!"

"Right. It's just for my first mission I was looking forward to a standard, unexciting, routine haulage job. For a few years. You know, more routine, less threat of violent death." The truth of the matter was, Daisy had been relying on her first couple of missions being nondescript and straightforward. This mission was the last thing she needed. She had planned on being unnoticed but this mission had shoved her into the centre of a bloody big spotlight accompanied by a carnival dancing band complete with garish attire and trumpets.

"But that's just it," the admiral's eyes gleamed, "no one is going to suspect a Yerbootsian ambassador of travelling on a garbage freighter. You'll be perfectly safe. He is listed on the crew manifest as the new science officer by the way."

"Science officer? Why do we need a science officer?"

"Well, it was either that or toilet attendant and they vetoed that suggestion on the basis that toilet attendants aren't bridge officers."

"Nonsense, he could control toilet functions from

the bridge, he wouldn't have to actually be in main toileteering."

"Well, in any case it's settled."

"I still think another ship would be better placed —"

"Daisy, we have had no contracts for months now. The ship is falling apart. We need the money. We just can't compete with the bigger players. But all that is about to change. In return for our part in this historic endeavour, we will receive exclusive and lucrative contracts."

"But —"

"Exclusive."

"Yes, but —"

"Lucrative."

"Dad? DAD?"

The admiral's eyes lost focus as he rolled his two favourite words around. "Lucrative . . . exclusive," he mumbled.

Daisy gave up. She was not going to get out of this. Fine. A plan came to mind. She would play the part of a distant and demanding leader and surreptitiously get the XO to do all the captain stuff until the ambassador was on his way. That's what XOs were for wasn't it, doing the work?

"OK Dad, you're right. Sounds exciting."

"Ah Daisy, if only your mother were here to see this. She would have been so proud."

"Do you think?" said Daisy through a sudden lump in her throat.

"Yes. However, she's not here and is probably getting drunk in a bar somewhere or sleeping with strangers. Or both."

"Lovely," said Daisy. "Talking of mum, don't you think it's about time you got out again? You've been alone for way too long."

"Me? Oh, don't worry about me. I have Carl."

"Carl?"

The admiral indicated the reddish-brown splat of hair currently sipping milk from a saucer on his desk.

"Oh, your . . . friend," said Daisy, not quite sure which word to use.

"If you mean 'wig', say wig," suggested the admiral.

"Fine. Wig."

"Oh, that's right, kick a man when he's down! I had to sell my hair just to keep the lights on young lady! Electricity isn't free!"

"It's solar-powered, Dad, the local star provides more than enough energy for this space station."

"Well, food then."

"Pseudo food is perfectly nutritious. Everyone eats it."

"Reconstituted faecal matter!"

"Delicious, reconstituted faecal matter." Daisy waved her hand at the Cakes 9000 unit in the corner, its lights indicating it had a splendid meal ready for heating and consumption. The tubing snaked away from the kitchen unit and into the lavatory compartment. "Face facts, Dad, you didn't need to sell your hair."

"Didn't need? Didn't need? How else can I afford to buy these smart wigs?"

"That's just the point. You buy them for company. Why don't you just make yourself available?"

"Available? Do you mean that I should become a prostitute?" he boomed.

Daisy picked up a leaflet from a stack on the desk. It showed the admiral in skimpy underwear and black fishnet stockings, striking a pose that would on anyone else be described as 'suggestive' but in his case could only be described as 'suggestive of the sort of thing that would get you in the night if you didn't eat your reconstituted faecal matter greens'. She held up the leaflet with a raised eyebrow.

"Yes, well that didn't work out. And put down that raised eyebrow before you break it."

Daisy returned both items to the desk.

The mass of hair growled. The admiral stroked it lovingly. "There there Carl, she doesn't mean it. Anyway," he returned his attention to Daisy, "You're not in any position to lecture me on relationships. What was the name of that horny one? The one from that planet where they all look like Satan. All red skin, fangs and horns."

"Satyr Seven. And his name was Philip."

"He really got my goat."

"He apologised for that."

"Apologised? Daisy, he ate my pet goat!"

"That's what they eat on Satyr Seven. He thought you were honouring the customs of his people."

The admiral huffed. "And what about that bloody hippy, new romantic, or whatever he was."

"Jack. And he was a poet."

"Oh yes, violent Jack 'the butcher' McVitie. 'Oh Daisy, I shall give you my heart'."

Daisy shifted uncomfortably. "Well, he did. It was in a nice box and everything."

"And then you dated the entire Hyperspatial Minotaur Hive!"

"Oh, come on, that was a rebound! Anyway, any of them were preferable to Michigan Jones."

"Who? Oh yes, that last one. What was wrong with him?"

"He had a nasty habit of being right."

"Bastard. Whatever happened to him?"

"Probably still lying drunk in his own filth."

"Huh. No ambition, eh?"

"Oh no, he had plenty of ambition, his ambition being to get drunk and lie in his own filth. From that point of view, he's a high achiever."

"Not captain material, though?"

"Definitely not."

"What about EO?"

"EO? What's EO?"

"Executive Officer."

"That's XO."

"No, it isn't. That would be Xecutive Officer. That's not how you spell Executive."

"No, the acronym takes the second letter of the first word."

"Don't be silly Daisy, that's not how acronyms work. They're not based on phonetics. That's the point of them, they take the first letter of each word. Everyone knows where there are. Otherwise, the whole thing is load of US."

"US?"

"Bull Shit."

Daisy raised her eyebrows. "Well, anyway, you can't go around calling the first officer EO, everyone would think you were saying hello all the time. I'd say 'EO?', and he'd say 'Oh hello Captain', and I'd say "No not 'Hello EO', I meant 'EO?' . . . EO', and he'd probably say 'Is the Captain ill?', and then I'd have to say —"

"Yes, yes, yes, Daisy I get the point. Well, whatever the acronym, this Michigan Jones fellow wouldn't make a good one?"

Daisy, who was still trying to follow the EO conversation through in her head suddenly zoned back into the conversation, "What? Oh, him, no. Lazy bastard. It's why I left him in the end. I doubt he even noticed I'd gone. I left him a note, but he hated reading things, said reading was like jogging for the eyes, made him out of breath and sweaty."

"Oh," said the admiral, "Good." He drummed his fingers on the desk for a moment. "Well, anyway you're well off out of that one and now you're a fully fledged captain. All the details, mission brief, command codes and so forth are in here," he said, handing her a thick folder.

He sat back in his chair. "So, ready to make history?"

"Ready."

They both stood, and each briefly covered their eyes with their hands in the traditional Terran space fleet salute.

"Good luck, Captain Daryl."

"Thank you, Admiral Daryl."

As she left her father's office, Daisy wondered if she should have confessed to him exactly how she had managed to pass the captain's exam. Not to worry, she thought, I'll just have to rely on the XO until I get the hang of it.

As Daisy left his office, the admiral wondered if he should have told her he had enlisted Michigan Jones as her EO.

The starship Space Scrap 17 was, like most starships of its class, a starship. But there the resemblance ended. It was a cobbled together miss-match of technologies and ill-fitting bulk heads. A 'cut and shut' job was an ignominious trick used by disreputable used car salesmen on old Earth and described a practice where two fatally damaged vehicles are welded together to look like a single, perfectly safe and legitimate transport. In the case of Space Scrap 17 a better description would be a 'cut, blow up, what does this bit do, never mind just stick it on, oh my god anyone stupid enough to try to fly this is going to die horribly, I mean caveat emptor doesn't really cover this does it, more like caveat horrendam mortam . . . and shut job'.

Assembled from the used spaceship lots of the

planet Yerboots, Space Scrap 17's construction consisted of ninety per cent welding and ten per cent shrug. As such, it was the only affordable vessel the Space Scrap company could afford. The admiral had taken advantage of a sales drive — buy one, get one free, by which the dealership meant, buy one fake certificate of flight worthiness, get something vaguely resembling a spaceship free.

Bargain.

Powered by exotic matter, its main propulsion, the wormhole generator, enabled the ship to journey between star systems. Admittedly, the length of the wormhole and therefore the amount of ordinary space it was able to circumvent at any one time was on the point-and-laugh end of the spectrum. Most starships contemporary with Space Scrap 17 were capable of generating much, much longer wormholes. Its Ion drive only just about qualified as an engine, which meant the speeds at which it could traverse the wormholes were best expressed in units of slow.

The main ship itself was a long, narrow affair with a bulbous front end containing the living quarters, bridge and various workaday areas. At the other end was a smaller bulbous section containing main engineering, wormhole generators and Ion drive.

Attached to the narrow connecting section were thirty squat oblongs which constituted the cargo bays. These could be separated from the main hull for remote loading and possessed their own propulsion systems. One of these, the largest, cargo bay one, was currently separated from the main hull and being loaded with raw sewage by another transport, thus keeping the disagreeable and messy process away from the space station with which Space Scrap 17 was now docked.

She carried a rag-tag crew of twenty and held a small complement of Some Blokes, biological robots printed when required. The rudimentary brains of these worker bees had only enough autonomous mental capacity required for completion of tasks requiring basic motor skills. Blokes could be deployed to complete non-specialist tasks considered either too menial or too dangerous for humans. In theory, you could easily run a ship with just a captain, an engineer and a crew of Blokes. The only limit on the number of Blokes you could have at any given time was the amount of pseudo-carbon blocks you could afford for the printer. In theory. However, there were minimum required crew sizes, depending upon the nature and purpose of the ship and without which you could not obtain a space worthiness certificate. So, much as the admiral would have preferred to crew his ship exclusively with Some Blokes, he had to pay for a minimal crew complement to stay in business.

Considerations such as these would understandably be on the mind of any bright, ambitious new XO on approach to his new ship.

Michigan Jones was, however, neither bright nor ambitious.

Or rather, he was both.

When he could be bothered, he was very bright, his mind capable of absorbing many facts and of joining the dots between seemingly unconnected events to discern the true pattern of things. This skill annoyed him immensely. Because his ambition moved in one direction only – his desire to be left alone to consume vast quantities of whatever dubious substance happened to be within arm's reach.

He didn't want to think.

He didn't want to 'do' things.

He didn't want to achieve anything.

You came into the universe with nothing and you left with nothing.

Achievers, freeloaders, prize-winning scientists, entrepreneurs, hippies, criminals, filing clerks, everybody everywhere ultimately got the same reward for their efforts . . . or lack thereof.

The rewards of life, Jones considered, were zilch. Bugger all.

Nothing.

So, what was the point of making an effort when you would ultimately get the same reward as the guy who built a vast business empire by slavishly working 24/7/365, or whatever your local day / month / year cycle might be?

Jones did not believe in an afterlife, despite what the various Aspirational Concepts tried to sell.

The only logical conclusion then was hedonism — you are born, have as much fun as you possibly can, you die. Simple.

The fact that the only reason he reached this conclusion was because he had a clever analytical brain was a matter of irritation to him. It reminded him he was capable of reasoning and reducing complex concepts to simple, readily understandable ideas. Which meant he was clever and really ought to do something with it. But his overriding ambition was to have no ambition. An oxymoron, the quiet voice at the back of his mind would point out. Fuck off, the loud voice at the front of his mind would respond.

Jones was convinced that he had in fact been twins, himself lazy and unfocused, the other full of buzz and intelligence. He was also convinced that he had absorbed his twin in the womb because the bright, optimistic, action-oriented other had disturbed his sleep. Bearing in mind humans only get nine months in their entire life where they are encouraged to sleep continuously and where they remained beyond the reach of other people, Jones Major was not inclined to give up any of that precious time. So, he concluded, he must have eaten his twin. In utero. He could find no other way to account for a personality so diametrically opposed to itself.

Jones turned to the pilot of the shuttle. "We should be there by now, why are you pissing about? I'm so bored I'm starting to mull. I hate mulling. Why are you making me mull?"

The pilot regarded him with a puzzled look. "You want to go direct?"

"Yes, I want to go direct."

"We can go direct. You want to make love?"

Jones blinked. "Yes, that was certainly direct. But no, I want to go directly to . . . " he gestured vaguely at the view screen, "the thing, the floaty space thing."

"Oh."

"Interesting accent by the way. And you have," he gestured around his face and body, "Gills. Lots of gills. Is that normal where you come from?"

"I am from Shoal Home. We are descended from fish."

"Well so am I but if I have any gills they are at best vestigial. I mean what do they do? They don't have any function in an oxygen atmosphere. They're just . . . distracting."

"We are, how do you say, bisexual."

"OK?"

"Yes, we spend half our life cycle in water, half on land."

Jones gave her a flat look. "Amphibious. Not bisexual."

"Amphibious? Does that mean you have a strong desire to have sex whenever you see an ocean?"

"Ah. No. That would be . . . amphibi-sexual. Or strange. Or something. I suppose swimming baths are very popular on Shoal Home?"

"Ooh," she flashed him a smile that would have been flirty were it not for the gills competing with her mouth for facial real estate, "Dirty bitch."

"Are we there yet?" asked Jones, desperately trying to change the subject, "Why is this taking so long?"

"You are part of command staff for Space Scrap 17?"

"Yes. Executive officer. Which I'm hoping means I get to tell people what to do and then they bugger off and leave me alone. What's that got to do with anything?"

"It's just that command staff usually like to take the long way around so they can get a good look at their new ship. Their eyes go all sort of glazed and they get this awestruck look on their face. Really weird. The beauty pass, they call it."

Jones peered at the view screen, "More like an ugly pass in this case."

"You don't seem the command type."

"I'm not. I'm the sitting in a chair getting drunk on a huge bottle of Big Papa's Big Papa Secretions and reading a book type."

"So why —"

"It was either this or a hospital."

"You're a medic?"

"No, I owe a lot of money to some nasty people and if I don't pay them, I'll end up in a hospital."

"Gangsters?"

"Booksellers and distilleries mainly. This gig was all I could get. And they have a very relaxed attitude about criminal records. The pay's not great but it's free rent and food and it's healthier if I don't stay in one place for too long."

The pilot pressed a few buttons and the sound of the engines fell away. She pulled out a well thumbed magazine and began flicking through it.

"What," said Jones, "what's going on, why have we stopped?"

"Holding pattern," she replied absently. "We have to wait fifteen minutes before we can dock with the ship."

"Great. Tremendous," muttered Jones. "What are you reading?"

She held up the periodical. '*Galactic Geographic — Hot, Salty Water Worlds Special, With Extra Pictures And Everything*,' read the title.

"My name is Marina. Aqua Marina. You want to make love?"

Jones's mouth dropped open as he regarded her face's gill clusters, which were now quivering slightly. Jones Minor, he knew, would say that this was a bad idea.

"Well," he said, unbuckling his seat belt, "You sirens have certainly sharpened up your act since ancient Greece, I must say. Pleased to meet you Marina," they shook hands. "Michigan Jones, hedonist."

As he leaned across, he resisted the urge to shout "Thar she blows!" He was nothing if not a class act.

#

Second Officer Steve Power waited nervously outside the shuttle bay. This was nothing unusual, he had a number of people smuggling things for him and he would often have to wait for them to come through disinfection and customs. However, the customs process on this ship was not a cause for concern. Their customs custom was to not look too closely at what people were bringing aboard. No, what was unusual today was that Steve was feeling nervous, an emotional state he was not used to. Despite his ridiculously butch second name, his demeanour and standard state of excitement were more akin to what one would expect from a flatlining patient in a hospital.

But today was full of potential worries. A new captain, a new XO, and a new science officer, all in one hit. Also, why the hell did they need a science officer? You could never tell what you were going to get with these command positions. Usually they were pushy little bastards. They'd start out wanting to make their mark, only to come aboard and discover that there were way too many marks on this ship already, most of them of a distinctly unsavoury nature. Then they'd file for a transfer and sod off at the earliest opportunity. But in the meantime, they would make life hell for the crew, instigating all sorts of 'new procedures' and 'more efficient ways of working' and 'clean that up before it evolves'. Ugh.

Steve had his back to the shuttle bay door when it opened.

"Hello beautiful, XO Michigan Jones reporting for duty."

Steve smiled. Well, that was one new command officer he didn't have to worry about.

He turned, a broad smile on his face, which is where he liked to keep it. His smile dropped.

His old drinking buddy Michigan Jones stood before him, looking just as he remembered. Except for . . .

"The slime. You're slimy now. Is that a fashion thing or a disease or . . ."

Jones looked down at himself, "What, this, well it's, no, never mind."

Steve sniffed the air, "Can you smell fish?"

"Yeah, the shuttle pilot, she was from Shoal Home, amphibi-sexual, something. We . . . it's complicated."

Steve collected his wits. "Right, well, welcome aboard Space Scrap 17!"

"Thanks. Where's my digs, I want a shower before I ingratiate myself to the captain. Is he or she or it aboard yet?"

"She, human and no."

"Good, I hate meeting new people. Well, I hate meeting people. I hate people. Time-wasting bastards. Especially captains. Especially, specifically new captains. They look at you like you're dirt!"

"Well, you are covered in fish slime. You might want to forgo the shower for a bit though. We've got a problem."

"Oh, flaps, not a problem! Listen Steve, I am determined to make my mark on this ship —"

Here we go, thought Steve.

"— and the first mark I want to make is a new rule about problems. Rule one — don't bring me problems Second Officer, bring me alcohol and a delicious biscuit. Or a comfy pillow. Or a delicious pillow and a comfy biscuit. I don't mind. But bring me alcohol."

Steve was not surprised at Jones's reaction. He had long since gotten used to his friend's outbursts of childish petulance at the first sign of anything that required effort. "Jeebuzz it's good to see you, old friend. It must be . . ."

"Must it?"

". . . five years?"

"Oh god yeah, that luxury cruise starship." Jones smiled at the memories. "You remember that stint we had in the kitchens?"

Steve laughed, "Yes. We had some laughs, didn't we?"

"We certainly did. All that food hygiene nonsense."

"Yes. And then all the crew got food poisoning."

"Yeah."

"And they all died."

". . . yeah."

"And we had to steal a couple of the life pods before the cops arrived."

"Yeah. Who . . . whose idea was it to blow up the ship to hide the evidence?"

"No, we didn't do that on purpose. We didn't repressurise the ship-side air locks before we ejected. Explosive decompression."

"And they said those things were fool proof!"

"Yeah! We showed them!"

"Yes, yes we did . . . lucky we were still in dry-dock and the guests hadn't boarded yet . . . so anyway, this problem. Not to do with air locks or anything?"

"No. Our cargo bays have been loading the raw sewage that we're supposed to transport to Yerboots. All of the bays, bar one, have re-docked with us, but the treatment tank in cargo bay three has a blockage. Someone needs to dive in and unblock it."

"Pft. I wouldn't like to be the poor sap who has to swim around in raw sewage trying to find a blockage in zero visibility and — and you want me to do it, don't you?"

"Well, you're the XO. What better way to get in with the new captain than to come aboard and sort out a problem straight away?"

"Well how about this. I report to the new captain that I've dealt with it by firing the second officer and got Some Bloke to unblock the tank."

"None of the Blokes are waterproof."

"Well, you do it then."

"You just fired me."

"You're re-hired. Get in the tank."

"But that's not fair."

"Not fair, what do you mean not fair?"

"Well, I did a coin toss earlier and you lost."

"What? Liar? Which side was up?"

"Heads."

"Ah, damn it I would have chosen tails!"

"I know."

"Right. Bollocks. Come on then, let's get this over with. I knew this was going to be a shit job."

#

Daisy entered the bridge. She had been on Space Scrap 17 for all of twenty minutes and so far, she had not been impressed.

First, there was no one to greet her on arrival. Well, that was OK because she wanted to arrive incognito anyway — get a chance to see the ship and crew operating without realising who she was.

Second, she had followed the signs to the bridge only to find herself in the men's toilet. Someone aboard apparently had a sense of humour when it came to putting up directional signage.

Third, now that she had found the bridge, it was devoid of any personnel. Aside from one. A lone individual stood by one of the command stations. Garbed as it was in some sort of environment suit, she could not tell if this individual was human or alien. The environment suit itself resembled a collection of featureless, black triangles. There was a torso-sized inverted black triangle, upon which sat a smaller head-sized inverted black triangle. Where a neck, or some other connection between torso and head should be, there was just empty space. Huh. The arms and legs were long and thin and wrapped in what looked like bandages.

An understaffed bridge. So much for first impressions.

Daisy coughed politely. "Hello – where can I find the XO?"

The figure, who had been bent over a console, stood erect and faced her. "Dead," it said.

"Sorry what?"

"What?"

Daisy frowned and decided to try again. "I am looking for the executive officer."

The figure inclined its head segment. "The crew?"

Oh great, Daisy thought, an alien who had not been fitted with language transcribers. "Do you understand Galactix?" she asked in that slow and slightly louder than usual way that people ask questions in their own language of people who don't speak it.

"No, I was talking about comms. All channels are dead."

"So, where's the engineering maintenance team?"

"All dead."

"Oh my god."

"Ah, you must be the new Captain. Welcome aboard, I am Mic Vol your communications officer."

Daisy's jaw dropped. "Communications? You?"

"Apologies Captain, I was temporally distracted."

Jeebuzz. "The word, Communications Officer, is 'temporarily'."

"No, temporally. I was having a discussion with you in the future. This can happen if I do not concentrate."

"Sorry, what?"

"I do not originate from this dimension. My species perceive time in both a segmented and sequential fashion. Or rather we do in our own dimension, where it makes sense. In your dimension this can be rather . . . annoying. I can forget to anchor myself if I allow my mind to wander."

"Right. So, hang on, in the future someone ends up dead?"

"It would appear so."

"Who? No, when, when does this happen?"

"In ten minutes."

"What?"

"Or ten years. It is difficult to tell."

"So, to summarise, you were just having a conversation with me in the future but all you can tell me is that in the future someone dies."

"Yes."

Fat lot of use. "Great. I'm a Sagittarius, can you tell me what sort of day I'm having?"

"A Sagittarian? That would explain it. I had expected you to be a human."

"I am human — no wait, what do you mean 'that would explain it'? That would explain what?" Daisy took a slow breath. "Never mind, start again. Where is the XO?"

"Ah, he is currently dealing with a problem in cargo bay three."

"Already? Well at least someone is getting on with things. Excellent."

"Shall I inform him of your arrival?"

"No, I'll head on down there. I'd like to see my dynamic new XO at work."

#

When Daisy arrived at the cargo bay she found a handful of Blokes going about various menial duties, all of which seemed to have something or other to do with three gigantic tanks that occupied the whole floor. Beyond the fact that the tanks just stood there throbbing at each other, she could not discern their purpose.

Someone came down from the operations room, boots clattering on the metal stairs.

The chubby man approached Daisy, his clipboard content commanding his full attention. He had a balding pate, and what remained of his receding hair hung in wispy strands down to his shoulders. He stopped abruptly, coming to a halt just before he collided with her. He looked up, surprised.

"Oh, hello," he said.

"Hello," said Daisy.

"You are . . .?"

"I am what?"

"Here."

"Yes."

"Right, well lovely to meet you." His attention returned to his clipboard and he made to move off.

"I'm looking for the XO, I was told he is dealing with a problem of some kind."

"Yes. Not to put too fine a point on it, he's in the shit."

"Lovely. Well, I'm Daisy Daryl and I may be able to help."

"No thanks. I'll let him know you called though."

"Captain Daisy Daryl."

"Oh! Right! Sorry, yes, should have realised, sorry, lots of stuff happening, er, well I'm your second officer, Navigator Steve Power." Steve shuffled a bit then stood to attention and gave the space fleet salute.

Daisy returned the salute. "So, what are these things?" she gestured at the huge containers behind her.

"Those? Sewage treatment plants. We have to treat the raw sewage before delivery. It flows from the other cargo bays into these treatment processors and then it's filtered and pumped through to the empty bays."

"I see. And where is the XO?"

"Him? Well like I said, he's in the shit."

"Yes, Mr Power, I appreciate he is dealing with some challenging issues, but I would like to consult with him to formulate an action plan to resolve said issues and enable us to get underway and meet our schedule and therefore our obligations to our contract. So, where is he?"

At that moment a loud thumping filled the cargo bay accompanied by a loud screech of protesting metal. Daisy and Steve stepped back from the treatment processors, eyes wide.

"Oh my gods, is it going to blow?" Daisy had to

shout to make herself heard over the ear-splitting noise.

The noise halted as suddenly as it had started, and a number of lights sprang into life on the second and third containers.

A chute attached to the front of the first processor tank gurgled and spat various gobbets of nasty brown blobs onto the floor of the bay, splattering two of the Blokes who, oblivious to the commotion, continued their work without pause.

Then came a distant wail and clamour as something fell from the chute.

It landed in a stinking heap on the floor of the bay.

"Ow. Dear gods," came a muffled voice from inside the excrement covered diving suit.

Daisy made to assist whoever the poor guy was, but Steve laid a restraining hand on her arm. "No Captain, probably best if you don't."

The figure struggled to its feet, pulling off the diving helmet. "That was disgusting. Literally couldn't see for shit. Jeebuzz I'm going to ask, no, demand, I shall demand a massive pay rise for this and furthermore —" The figure froze as he caught sight of Daisy and Steve.

"Oh, er, XO," said Steve, "May I introduce the

new Captain. Captain Daisy Daryl, this is Michigan Jones, XO and sewage pipe unblocker."

"Captain?" said Jones. "Really?"

"Really," said Daisy.

"Oh," said Jones. "That's . . ."

"A surprise?" finished Daisy.

"Surprise yes. Awkward is also a word."

"I see your vocabulary has increased."

Jones stood in silence for a moment, excrement dripping from his suit.

"Right," he said. "Well, this is . . . this is a thing. So, I imagine you have lots of questions. Shouty questions. Recriminations, accusations, that sort of malarkey."

"Jones . . . Michigan," said Daisy, taking a step toward him. She halted as the stomach-churning stench of effluent hit her, thought better of it, and took two steps back. "I'm so sorry, how can you ever —" she was going to ask how he could ever forgive her, but the smell simply made her gag.

Steve looked at each of them in turn, uncertain of what was happening. "Oh good, you've met . . . hooray."

"Yes Steve," said Jones. "We've met. Well, more than met, we had a . . ."

"A relationship?" suggested Daisy.

"Yes. One of those."

"Oh great, then you'll get on really well," said Steve happily. "That's always a thing – will the new captain and XO like each other. Will they hate each other, you know, really get on each other's –"

"Steve, shut up," said Jones. "We had a 'relationship'. And it ended."

"Yes," said Daisy, looking at her feet and willing a hole to appear and swallow her up. She made a mental note to kill her father at the earliest opportunity.

"We had some pretty bad arguments towards the end," Jones said, watching Daisy closely.

"Bad arguments?" said Steve. He nodded, making a face as if imagining the vitriolic exchanges. "What, like vicious appeals to authority, tautologies, nasty bit of post hoc ergo propter hoc, that sort of thing?"

Jones gave him a flat look. "Not badly constructed arguments Steve . . . although to be fair they were mostly ad hominem by the end."

A tannoy burst into life, breaking the relationship horror standoff. "This is Mic Vol — the science officer is about to arrive at the shuttle bay."

"Well," said Daisy brightly, thankful for the diversion "I'd best go . . ." She gestured awkwardly at the door.

"Yes," said Jones, "I'm long overdue a shower and a change of clothes. I'll . . ." He gestured vaguely at the crew changing rooms.

"Yes," said Steve, "and I'll um . . ."

"Oh, shut up Steve," said Jones, just as a couple of Blokes approached and dutifully emptied their sterilisation spray units at him.

Jones disappeared from sight, cloaked in a swirling antibacterial fog.

Daisy made the most of it and left for the shuttle bay at speed.

DR OLGA SMIERT stood by the shuttle bay exit. She did not ordinarily greet new crew members this way, preferring instead to have them at her mercy in her laboratory — no, she corrected herself — she preferred to see them in sick bay for their preliminary medical check-ups as early as possible. For the sake of her true work, she must keep a check on her thinking. One small slip and she would be faced with angry crowds of agrarian peasants screaming about blasphemy and black magic and waving crudely shaped agricultural implements outside her cliff top windmill. Again. She shuddered at the memory.

"Doctor Smiert, I presume." A short, chubby, nondescript woman approached. Oh, how many ways you can die, thought Smiert. Which was her usual line of thinking upon meeting new people. She smiled.

"You clearly a good reader of people, yes?"

"Well, you know," replied the woman.

"You have telepathic strain in family? Ever had an ancestor accused of witchcraft? Have you had your ESP rating checked?"

The woman went all misty eyed. "Well, now you mention it, I did have an aunt who —"

"I only ask because otherwise I fail to see how you knew me to be Doctor Smiert. Because other than the regulation white medical jacket I am wearing, the somewhat clichéd stethoscope hanging around my neck and this lanyard showing my photograph with the words 'Dr Smiert — Chief Medical Officer' written underneath it, there is absolutely no way you could have known who I was."

The hobbit — for that is what the doctor had decided this thing was — blinked a few times. Its features hardened.

"Interesting bedside manner, Doctor. I'm Daisy Daryl. Captain Daisy Daryl. Which you couldn't possibly have known since I'm not wearing a badge with 'Daisy Daryl — Captain and Not Someone to Piss Off' written on it. Obviously, unlike some of us, you have no history of telepathy in your family. But there is that fatal genetic defect you have, you know, the mutated genome that causes fatal sarcasm. Perhaps you have ancestors who were brutally stabbed to death because of their fatal propensity to be a smart arse? Are you noting my frequent use of the word 'fatal' here, Doctor?"

So much for keeping a check on her thinking, "Ah, yes. Captain. My mistake. Busy day. Apologies."

"Accepted. So, what brings you to the shuttle bay?"

"I wish to meet the new science officer. A Yerbootsian. Interesting species, not one I have seen before."

"They're indistinguishable from humans, aren't they?"

Ah. She didn't know. Good. "Well Captain, I like to book medical check-up as early as possible for new crew. I was in area, so . . ."

"Very diligent."

"Yes. It is shame, last Captain was not so thorough."

"What happened to him?"

"I kill him. Accident. Ooops."

Daisy frowned. "Tell me again why my father employs you?"

"I am cheap. Can I book in your medical now?"

Smiert held a stylus poised over her DEVICE — a ubiquitous, compact computerised tool that was very cheap, very useful and interfaced with pretty much anything in technologically advanced societies. The word DEVICE was an acronym that stood for 'Personal Digital Apparatus'. Its inventor was really clever with digital technology but absolute rubbish with acronyms.

"Maybe later," said Daisy. "'Smiert', that's an interesting name."

"You think? It is quite common name in Mother Russia."

"Really? Does it mean anything?"

Smiert regarded the captain suspiciously. Was she trying to make a point? Was she, despite all appearances to the contrary, a cunning strategist and master manipulator, someone who in psychological terms would register high on the Machiavellian end of the Dark Triad scale?

"In my mother tongue, *Smiert* means 'happy', 'lovely' or 'kind'," Smiert lied.

"Oh. Sweet," Daisy smiled at her.

Smiert's suspicions chuckled to themselves and wandered off – clearly nothing to see here. The captain was an idiot.

Just then the door to the shuttle bay whooshed open and a figure walked through.

The two women gaped at the vision standing before them. All thoughts of the previous discussion were abruptly shoved from their minds as they tried to comprehend the epitome of loveliness now beaming at them. This would have been bad enough, but the fact that it was beaming at them from within the confines of a black leather cat-suit that lovingly hugged its voluptuous contours was just taking the piss.

"Please tell me she's not the new science officer. Please tell me she's not the new science officer. Please tell me she's not the new science officer," Daisy muttered.

"Hello, I'm the new Science Officer," said the new science officer.

"Bollocks," said Daisy.

Smiert smiled to herself. The captain had clearly never met a Yerbootsian before.

The new science officer was, frankly, gorgeous. Her figure was perfect. Her makeup and hair were immaculate. Her breasts could stun at a thousand paces. Her curvaceous hips hinted at the promise of many children. Her poise was that of a princess, not one of the stuffy old ones but one of the fresh, new, modern princesses with fresh, new, modern DNA that royal families have to accept from time to time just to temporarily stave off the relentless production of royal genetic monstrosities for another generation or two.

In short, she was every woman's nightmare. She was young, perfect and gorgeous.

Which, for all other women on the crew, was a massively unfair and cruel twist of fate. Looking at her every day would be like having to look in a magic mirror that constantly reminded you how imperfect and inadequate you were:

"Mirror, mirror on the wall, who's the fair —"

"NOT YOU, YOU UGLY BITCH!".

All of which would have been a problem if, in fact, the gorgeous creature that stood before them was a woman.

But he wasn't.

He was a perfectly formed, straightforwardly heterosexual, Yerbootsian male. Although to be fair, Smiert considered, she was making an assumption about his sexual orientation.

In the animal kingdom of Earth, the males are the gorgeous ones, the flamboyant ones, literally the peacocks. The males take fastidious care in how they look. The females, on the other hand, are dowdy, bland, wear the animal equivalent of beer-stained track suits, fart in public and consider belching the most amusing, if not the most sophisticated, form of communication. If they were able to conceive of them, they would consider shoes simply an item of clothing and not magical talismans of promise and rainbows that probably taste of chocolate. But when it comes to the human race the complete reverse is, by and large, true.

Evolution on the planet Yerboots decreed no such reversal. Their males, like the rest of their animal kingdom, are universally gorgeous, their females universally dowdy.

Since it was still the women who gave birth and breast-fed their offspring, Smiert found it puzzling as to why the men had such fantastic tits. But such intrigues could wait.

The science officer frowned at the two gawping women, which, annoyingly, only made him look more gorgeous.

"Ah, yes," Smiert broke the silence and held out her hand, "I am Doctor Smiert and this is Captain Daryl."

The captain continued to stare with that same unblinking, wide-eyed stare that rabbits reserve for the beams of car headlamps in the middle of the night. Smiert nudged her. "Hello," she said, snapping out of her reverie. "Your tits are amazing!"

Smiert coughed.

"No, sorry, no," the captain blustered, "No. Hello, you look amazing, welcome aboard."

"Er, thank you. My name is not pronounceable by your primitive Earth tongue."

"What?" Daisy glanced incredulously at Smiert with a triumphant look that seemed to say 'Aha — I knew it, she's a right bitch!'.

"My name is not pronounceable by your primitive Earth tongue," he repeated.

Smiert could almost feel the the captain bristle. "Now listen here young lady, we'll have none of that snooty phonetic superiority on this ship. You may have a name full of multiple syllables or coughs and whistles and clicks but I think you'll find we are perfectly capable of mastering someone's bloody name around here, thank you very much."

Just then a new voice broke into the discussion. "Hey, NotPronounceableByYourPrimitiveEarth-Tongue, you old bastard, how you doing? Heard you were coming aboard, good to see you again."

NotPronounceableByYourPrimitiveEarth-Tongue's face split into a broad, and of course gorgeous, smile, revealing perfect and of course gorgeous teeth. "Steve," he said, "Long time no see. Catch up later in the bar?"

"You bet!" said Steve. He nodded briefly at the others and continued on his way.

"Right," said Daisy, "Well, as I was saying NotPronounceableByYourPrimitiveEarthTongue, welcome aboard."

NotPronounceableByYourPrimitiveEarth-Tongue smiled. "Please, Captain, call me Tongue. NotPronounceableByYourPrimitiveEarthTongue is my formal name, only really used at family gatherings and the odd formal occasion. Or upon seeing someone for the first time after a prolonged absence, as you just saw."

"Right, so you know Steve of old then?"

"Oh yes, we've been friends for a long time. Off and on."

"Friends . . . so what, you and he had a thing?"

"We had some interesting times."

"What, sort of boyfriend or 'just friends'?"

"Boyfriend?" Tongue raised a quizzical and perfect eyebrow. "Oh, no, just drinking buddies really, I'm not gay. Is Steve gay? He never mentioned it."

A mixture of expressions wandered across the captain's face. Smiert could almost hear the squeaking of the mental wheels turning as she tried to process Tongue's comment. She decided to put her out of her misery before her brain shattered.

"Science Officer Tongue is a typical Yerbootsian male, Captain."

"He? Typical? Jeebuzz, what do the women look like!?"

"Excuse please Science Officer, the Captain is not familiar with Yerbootsian physiognomy — is what humans call 'ignorant bitch'. OK if we talk about you in the third person while I explain?"

"Ah," said Tongue gracefully, "yes, of course."

Smiert explained the concept of evolved peacock males to Daisy. Her face gradually cleared.

"Oh, Tongue, I do apologise. This commission has all been a bit of a whirl, I haven't had the chance to review the crew roster in enough detail. Please forgive my ignorance."

"Think nothing of it, Captain, I understand. Our physiognomy is something of a rarity in the galaxy."

"I'll say," said Daisy in a rush of relived bonhomie, "For a minute there I was going to make you sign a non-disclosure agreement with respect to your . . . your . . . to those." Daisy gestured vaguely around her chest.

"Right," said Tongue an uncertain smile on his lips.

Daisy realised she had again misspoken, but instead of changing the subject, just dug herself deeper. "Talking of which, why do you have boobs? Do all . . . men have boobs . . . like those . . . boobs?"

"They supply venom to our death quills," said Tongue flatly.

Daisy's face contorted in the sort of polite, uncertain expression that wasn't sure if it had heard correctly but didn't want to push it. She nodded and made a 'hmmm' noise.

"Would you like the contact code for our personnel complaints department?" offered Smiert.

"Why do people complain about your personnel department? Are they inefficient?" said Tongue.

"No but personnel seem to think it is sort of thing personnel departments should have."

"Sounds like a ludicrous waste of time."

"Yes. But most personnel departments are a ludicrous waste of time, made up of the sort of people who think they should have a complaints section. Makes them feel like they have a useful skill set."

"Oh. Well, what I would like," said Tongue, "is to get to my quarters and freshen up? Perhaps the

Captain would accompany me? We have much to discuss."

"Yes," said Daisy brightly, at last finding a combination of words in the conversation she understood, "Quarters. Yes. Doctor," she nodded at Smiert and led Tongue away.

Alone now, Smiert chuckled to herself. She could of course have explained all this to the captain ahead of time and saved her blushes, but she was bored, and it had been a while since she had had a laugh. Not since the demise of the last captain, in point of fact. He, unlike Daisy Daryl it seemed, had had a clever and suspicious mind, the sort of suspicious mind that asked too many questions. Questions like, "That isn't loaded is it?"

JONES GAVE an annoyed grunt and shouted, "Sod off!" at the door.

Having showered off and burnt the sewage-covered diving suit, he had made his way to his cabin only to find that the shuttle bay had misplaced his luggage. Steve had rustled up a mishmash of clothing for him to wear while they hunted for his belongings — a pair of boots, camouflage trousers and a black T-shirt bearing the image of a cartoon zebra wearing a big cheesy grin and a mane that resembled the long hair of a messiah-like prophet, emblazoned with the slogan 'Cheer yourself up, punch a zebra in the face'. Odd, although apt considering the circumstances, he thought.

And now, after a decidedly unpleasant start to his new commission, he finally got to sit with his thoughts and a can of his favourite beverage, Big Papa's Big Papa Golden Secretions (golden secretions being the premium product of the secretions brand — he made a mental note to ask Steve for the name of his supplier).

The door chime sounded again.

"Sod off!" he shouted at it again.

The door opened. "Oh bloody hell, what now, go away, I'm not on duty, I'm dead, sod off whoever you —" his voice froze as he stood to face his persecutor.

The door slid shut behind Daisy. Or rather, it slowly squealed shut in an angry mechanical protest. She tried to ignore its protracted screams.

"Oh," said Jones, "It's you."

She smiled. "Hello —" The door, which had not fully closed, gave another squeal as it juddered across the last two inches and finally came to a rest against the frame. Daisy pursed her lips. She paused for a moment and then tried again. "Hello Michigan, it's been a long —" she stopped suddenly, her eyes wide with horror. "Jeebuzz, where are your legs!" she screamed.

Jones looked down. "Oh, yeah, right." He slapped his right thigh and the camouflage trousers switched off, revealing their un-camouflaged state as a pair of beige slacks. They were ex-military kit. Ex because although battle hardened, tough soldiers liked the idea of clothing that could render them invisible to the enemy, they baulked at the thigh-slapping mechanism for switching them on and off, which had the unfortunate effect of making the whole troop look like they were extras in a blood drenched pantomime. This, they considered, was something of a mood killer. Not that they objected to the killing part, it's just that they worked really hard to create the right atmosphere while on killing sprees and this thigh-slapping nonsense was just not on.

Jones and Daisy regarded each other in an awkward silence.

"So," he said.

"So," she said.

"You're looking well . . . Captain."

"As are you, XO."

Another silence.

"So," she said.

"So," he said.

"Here we are," she said.

Jones shook himself, "What am I thinking, come in Daisy, make yourself comfortable, would you like a drink?" he waggled the can, "I'm sure I can find a glass or a cup or a shoe . . ."

"Still drinking the Big Papa, eh? I'll pass thank

you." Daisy moved further into the room. "Interesting T-shirt."

"What this? Oh, yeah shuttle bay seems to have lost my bags, so Steve found me some stuff."

"'Punch a zebra'. Reminds me of when we first met."

"Ah yes," said Jones, "In the zebra enclosure of the zoo on Apoplexia Three. I was drunk and shouting abuse at the zebras: 'What's with the stripes? Make up your bloody mind!' and all that . . ."

"And I arrived and thought 'oh, he's a keeper'."

"I never knew that — one glance and you thought I had boyfriend potential?"

"No, I meant the man who was wrestling you to the ground . . . he was a . . . zookeeper."

"Right. Yes, of course. Well, I was too technically, no, actually, it was my first day on the job. And last as it turned out. God, I fucking hate zebras. Equine barcodes. Pretentious bastards."

The awkward silence returned.

'Do you remember what I taught you, SoulKin?' Daisy thought at Jones dreamily, *'Can you still sense my thoughts?'*

Jones's eyes narrowed. "What?" he demanded. "Why are you staring at me? Stop it, your eyes have gone all glassy and weird you strange bitch. I need the toilet."

Her shoulders dropped slightly. She was sure that would work on someone, someday. Ah, well. "Right, no, anyway, the mission —" she began to say but then stopped.

'Of course he can't hear you, neither of you are telepathic,' said a voice in Daisy's head.

'Wait, what? Who is this?' Daisy thought back at it.

'Oh shit she heard us!' there was a strange receding, scuttling noise that wasn't a noise and then the voice in her head was gone. Daisy got the distinct impression of beetles. She shook herself. Whatever.

"We should talk about the mission."

"Yes. The mission," said Jones.

Daisy opened her mouth to continue. Jones raised his hand. "Wait, Daisy. Before the, the mission and the stuff and all that, don't you think we should address the elephant in the room?"

Daisy smiled uncertainly. "Yes, yes I suppose so."

Jones turned away, "Errol, would you mind?" he said to the elephant sitting in the corner of the room eating buns.

Errol, a crewman from a humanoid *Elephantidae*

species, paused his munching. "Oh, right. OK. Can I take the buns?"

"Yeah, yeah," Jones waved a dismissive hand, "Thanks for the help with the furniture and stuff."

"Oh, no problem," said Errol. "Lovely buns."

Errol nodded briefly to them both and, still munching, left the cabin.

"OK so, the mission and the stuff?" said Jones once they were alone and the door had screamed itself shut again.

Daisy recounted the details of the mission; the Yerbootsian ambassador posing as science officer, the transport of sewage, the rendezvous with the LASS Square Jaw, the vague interest of the Ululations.

Jones sat in silence for a moment. "Blimey," he said eventually. "Well, good luck with that and everything," he said, standing abruptly, "This was a nice chat, but I have packing to do and shuttles to be on."

"Wait, what, you've only just arrived!"

"I didn't sign up for missions of daring doo-doo and square jaws and, what was the phrase you used, oh yeah, 'violent death'. I resign."

"Jones, I need you!"

"No you don't, you're a Captain now. Get Steve or one of the Blokes or a vending machine to be XO, you'll be fine!"

"I won't."

"Yes, you will. This is what you and your lunatic dad always wanted wasn't it? To boldly go and violently die? Not my cup of Big Papa Secretions, not by a long shot. You wanted to do things, well this is a thing and you're doing it, you're Captain."

"I'm not."

Jones began moving around grabbing things seemingly at random. "Where's my spleen, I'm sure I left it somewhere. Under a cushion maybe —" the frenetic motion suddenly stopped. He gave Daisy a flat look. "Not. What?"

For a moment, Daisy's hands wrestled with each other. She took a deep breath and forced them to her sides.

"I'm not a captain. Not really."

Jones's lips pursed. "Eph-hain" he said.

"What?"

Jones un-pursed his lips. "Explain," he repeated.

"I, uh," Daisy's hands were wrestling again. She looked around the room. She mumbled something.

"What?"

She mumbled again.

"Daisy you're going to have to speak in frequencies other than the ones that only dogs can hear. What did you say?"

She met his eyes. "I said I cheated the exam!" she shouted.

Jones's jaw dropped. Then he laughed. "Oh no. No, no, no, no, no."

"Yes, yes, yes, yes, yes. Jones, I had to pass, I failed it seventeen times before! Other parents drop subtle hints about how lovely it would be to have grandchildren but no, all my Dad wants is a fleet of spaceships and his only child sitting in the captain's chair on the flag-ship. I had to do something!"

"See, I told you, didn't I? What did I tell you?"

"Smelling your own farts is morally acceptable, smelling someone else's is sick."

"No, the other thing, I said the other thing. Ambition is natural selection's way of weeding out assholes and risk takers from the gene pool."

"It'll be fine, we'll get through."

"Quote 'If certain factions discover we have a Yerbootsian ambassador aboard they will immediately brutally murder the ambassador and anyone who comes into contact with him'. Unquote."

Daisy waved her hand dismissively. "I was exaggerating."

"Yes, you've done a lot of that recently, haven't you Daisy? Like when you said you'd passed the captain's exam."

"Talking of which, XO, since this is a mission briefing it's not Daisy, it's Captain. And I refuse your resignation."

"That's the point though isn't it, it's not 'Captain' it's 'exam cheat'. Wait," Jones thrust a finger at her. "How did you cheat the exam? You can't cheat the exam, it goes on for days, there are simulations and brain scans and people poking you with bugger sticks and everything."

"I . . ."

"Yeeees?"

"I bought a temporary mind patch from the Dark Market. I bought the persona of Captain Weaver."

"Captain Ripley Weaver?" breathed Jones incredulously. Captain Ripley Weaver, Earth's first starship pilot who, due to an unfortunate encounter with a murderous extraterrestrial endoparasitoid xenomorph early in her career, developed an irrational hatred of anything not human and went on an insane killing spree across the galaxy.

Daisy nodded reluctantly, "I came top of the class in Mission Management with a distinction in Xenophobia."

"Seriously? Daisy I have no need to tell you how incredibly dangerous that is."

"No, you don't."

"Daisy that's incredibly dangerous."

"I know. You don't need to tell me."

"You are aware of how incredibly dangerous mind patches are?"

"Yes," repeated Daisy through gritted teeth, "you have no need to tell me how incredibly dangerous they are."

Jones thought for a moment. "They're incredibly dangerous."

"I was desperate, I had to do something. Besides I'm pretty sure I know it all, it's just I'm rubbish at exams. And anyway, I'm still sane."

"Says the woman who cheated her captain exams with incredibly dangerous technology and accepted an incredibly dangerous mission involving competing factions of bloodthirsty Galactic zealots." Jones slumped down into a chair. "Wow," he said. He felt numb. She had used a mind patch? From the Dark Market? Not only were such things dangerous but they were also ethically dubious – not to mention illegal. Decades ago, it had been expensively fashionable to digitally upload the minds of the great and the good to advanced computers. Anyone able to afford the extortionate prices could use a mind patch to download their choice of celebrity dead person directly to their own brain. The practice had soon fallen from favour due to technical difficulties, the main technical difficulty being that mind patches had a nasty habit of turning their users totally insane. The developers had known about this, of course, but as they were early adopters of the product, they were insane enough to bring it to market. Mind patches were quickly outlawed and the suppliers shut down. But copies of the digital personas became available for cheap on the Dark Market along with DIY versions of the neural upload technology. Anyone caught with a neural uploader faced a long prison sentence and a hefty fine. Jones frowned. Or was it a hefty prison sentence and a long fine?

"Look forget about the mind patch. Jones . . . Michigan," Daisy sat in the chair opposite him. "I know I said some horrible things in that letter. It was wrong and cowardly, but I've grown a lot as a person since then and I would never do such a thing again. You have every reason to hate me but . . . Michigan, I need you."

"Letter? What letter? How dare you say horrible things to me in that letter. How could you be so callous and cruel? Where is it, I want to read it so I can be offended and . . . righteously indignated!"

"Well, I don't have it, I left it with you. On the kitchen table. That morning . . . when I left you."

Jones often had trouble following what Daisy was saying but this conversation was a doozy. It was one of things he had mentioned in that letter he wrote to her that morning when he walked out . . . wait.

"Daisy, when you left that letter on the kitchen table, did you . . . did you by any chance notice another letter?"

"What?" she frowned, "Well now you come to mention it . . . yes, yes I think there was one. I was in such a hurry to leave I didn't take much notice and . . . Jones?"

It was Jones's turn to look around the room.

"Jones, what was in the other letter?"

"Well, you started it, you wrote a horrible letter to me and ended our relationship, so I did it first."

"WHAT?" Daisy stood, her fists balled at her sides, "Are you telling me you walked out on me!"

"Yes, yes, I walked out on you!" Jones stood to face her.

"Oh no you didn't Michigan Jones, because I walked out on you! Don't you go trying to claim walkage! I'm the walker, you are the walkee!"

"Rubbish, my letter was there first! Oh yes, you don't like it that your walkee walked before he became a walkee and so proved himself a walker!"

"Yes Jones, there we can agree because you, sir, are a MASSIVE walker!"

"Well, you seem to have made your position quite clear. I think I should leave now."

"This is your cabin."

"I think I should stay now."

The conversation thus brutally murdered, they just stood and glared at each other. The tannoy thankfully broke the glare off. "Captain to the bridge. We are clear to leave space station orbit."

"That means we can leave. In case you didn't get that, what with not really being a captain and all."

"I know what it means Jones. And once we've completed this mission you can leave as soon as you like."

"Really? I'm not sure I understood that. Why don't you write it down in a letter for me?"

"Bridge. Now." Daisy turned and stomped toward the door.

Jones followed. Their stomping was interrupted for several moments while the door went through its tortuous ritual of squealing slowly open, during which time they stood silently clenching and unclenching their jaws and glaring at it.

Finally, the door was open.

Daisy stomped off left.

Jones stomped off right.

"The bridge is this way — Captain." shouted Jones.

Daisy did a prompt about face and stomped after him, wishing she was stomping his stupid face instead.

#

On the bridge, Steve Power sat at the navigation console. He shook his head. "I still think these coordinates will make our ETA at Yerboots too early. Unless you're planning to make a quick stop off along the way, ha ha."

Tongue gave a strangled laugh. He wondered if his old friend knew more than he was letting on and considered killing him. Then he decided that killing him was probably overkill. And a tad neurotic. No, Steve was just good at his job. Something of a rarity aboard this ship.

"To be honest," Tongue leaned in close, "I'd like to take a look at an interesting binary star system with a planet in stable eccentric orbit that's on our way. I'm going to ask the captain but if she says no, I'll point out that it won't make us late and we'll have plenty of time." Tongue winked conspiratorially at Steve, who nodded and returned a sly smile.

Tongue straightened. "Although, speaking of being late, shouldn't she be here by now?"

"Yes, sorry about that," said Daisy, stomping onto the bridge, "Our XO doesn't know his way around quite as well as he pretends."

Jones followed Daisy onto the bridge. "On my last ship the bridge was where I expected it to be. Alright, so apparently on this ship, that's where the galley is. Ridiculous. Who puts a galley there? That's where bridges should go."

"Second Officer, what's our status?" Daisy asked Steve as she settled into the captain's chair.

"What? Oh, well, I'm . . . here, and you're there and —"

"Ship's status Mr Power, stat!"

"What?"

"Mr Power, when I say stat, I mean Stat!"

Steve looked confused, on the verge of panic. He pointed at his coffee mug. "You mean stiss?"

"Stat!"

"Stat's my coffee mug!"

Jones took up position at his station, slightly behind and to the left of Daisy's chair. The command positions made a 'V' shape, rather like that of migrating geese. Except without the feathers or the wings. Or the geese. The command posts were XO, captain and mission ops. The mission operation station was not always occupied as regular tasks could be managed by the XO. Jones made a mental note to ensure the mission ops station was always occupied. "Steve, she means she wants it now, as in straight away."

"Oh," said Steve, looking even more confused. He picked up his coffee mug and, holding it before him like a supplicant, walked it over to Daisy.

"Not," called Jones, "the mug. She wants to know the current situation with respect to the ship and the stuff and all the bollocks that's going on."

Steve's head twitched between Jones and Daisy. Daisy massaged the bridge of her nose with her thumb and index finger.

"Right," said Steve, looking relieved. He loved that coffee mug. He returned to his station.

"Beg pardon," said Mic Vol from the comms station, "but would that information not normally come from the mission operations station? Or the XO in the event the ops station is vacant?"

"Yes," said Jones causally as his hands worked to reconfigure his display console to a format more to his liking. "But I'm sure the Captain knows that."

Daisy turned slowly in her seat to aim a deadly glare at Jones. "Status," she said through gritted teeth, "Stat."

A new voice broke into the conversation. "All bar one of the cargo pods have returned to main body. Sewage treatment underway. Last of the pods is ready to dock with us. Flight clearance issued from space station."

Jones looked up from his console to regard the owner of the voice. Standing at mission ops, Tongue met his glance and nodded. Jones felt a hot flush creep up his body.

"Thank you, Science Officer," said Daisy, her gaze still fixed on Jones.

"Michigan Jones," Jones introduced himself, "XO."

"You can turn off the charm, such as it is," said Daisy, "He's immune." She turned back to face the main viewer.

"That's a lie, I'm not immune, and the Science Officer can be as charming to me as she likes."

"Science Officer Tongue is a 'he', XO," said Daisy, flatly.

Jones, nonplussed, looked over at Tongue who smiled and nodded.

"Right, OK, welcome aboard Mister . . . Tongue."

"Thank you, XO. Pod ready to dock," repeated Tongue.

Jones shook himself. "Yes, right, initiate docking auto-sequence."

"No." Daisy turned once more to glare at Jones. "Our new XO will perform the docking sequence . . . manually."

"Captain is that wise?" said Tongue.

"Why not, our XO seems to have all the answers so far. You are qualified for manual docking, Mr Jones?"

"No."

"Good, then it's settled. You should get some practical experience."

"As XO it is my duty to present the Captain with alternative options and strategic assessments. May I respectfully suggest that this strategy is a ridiculously and unnecessarily dangerous one? The sort of command only an idiot would issue. Or someone who hasn't passed her captain's exam? Thus, I present the alternative option of sod off you crazy bitch."

"Come now XO, I have every faith in your abilities," Daisy smiled sweetly at him.

"What are you talking about?" said Tongue, his

eyes flicking gorgeously between Daisy and Jones. "This is an important mission, we cannot —"

"The XO is simply squirming, Mr Tongue. It's OK Jones, just a test to see if you are up to being XO. I can always have a Bloke printed if you don't feel up to it . . . in the meantime Tongue, set for auto dock."

"Oh no you don't!" Jones roared. "I'm not having that." Jones stomped around to stand behind Steve. "Steve, let's have the cargo pod on main viewer!"

"What, you're really doing this?"

"Yeah, I know what I'm doing trust me. I saw a manual once."

"Oh right, you've read the manual on the procedure."

"Yeah. Well, no, reading manuals makes my eyes scream. I saw one. It looked simple. Shut up. Put the thing on main viewer. Stat."

Steve boggled. "OK, cargo pod on screen. I expect you'd like to see a tactical overlay," he said hopefully, "So you can monitor trajectory and dangerous proximity to the ship's hull and projected death count and so on?"

"Nah, who needs it. We should go to dramatic alert though."

"Dramatic alert, aye." Steve stabbed at a button. Immediately, the bridge lighting decreased, faces of the bridge officers and their consoles lit only by red emergency lights.

"Hang on, no, I can't see anything. Turn the lights back up."

"Dramatic alert cancelled."

The lighting returned to its usual soulless sodium-based levels.

Jones looked around, not happy with the lack of atmosphere. "Oh, I know, lens flare. Have we got any lens flare?"

"The cargo bay is getting quite close to the hull. And by 'quite' I mean 'catastrophically'."

"Right, fine, let's do it without lens flare. OK fire bay manoeuvring thrusters. Half power. That's it. Watch the velocity. Adjust pitch, negative three degrees."

"Oh sorry," Steve adjusted his trousers and sat up straighter.

"Watch your roll angle."

"My what?"

"Adjust yaw by five tacks."

"Wait, what's a 'tack'?"

"Retract rollocks."

"You're just making it up . . ."

"That's it. Velocity zero, thrusters off. Inertia should do the job now." Jones stepped back, a satisfied smile on his face. Not bad, he thought, not bad at all.

All around the bridge people started breathing again.

They watched the main viewer as cargo bay one gracefully approached its docking port. They continued watching as it gracefully crashed into its docking port, elegantly bounced off again and poetically skidded along the hull, destroying a horrifyingly large amount of external equipment as it did so, before finally colliding with, and coming to rest on, the engineering section.

Jones turned to Daisy. "Cargo bay one manual docking complete, as requested Captain. The Captain was clearly correct in ignoring the perfectly reasonable alternative options her XO presented in pursuit of her own petty agenda. Well done. You can't learn these raw decision-making skills at captain school, this is the sort of intuitive thinking one has to be born with. The XO would like to thank the Captain for her faith in his abilities."

Daisy gave him a flat look. "You are such a dick," she said.

Jones smiled and strode back to his command station, content with a job well done.

The rest of the bridge crew continued to gape at

the screen, which showed various bits of Space Scrap 17 spinning off into space.

#

If the crew of Space Scrap 17 had not been occupied with desperately trying to save what remained of their ship, some of them might have noticed a newscast playing out on various unwatched monitors around the ship. This is what it said:

"This is Galactic News [INSERT NUMBER OF HOURS IN YOUR LOCAL DAY CYCLE]".

"Hello, I'm male newsbot. In a dramatic twist today, my ankle is now in a cast. In other dramatic twists, Leroy Cakes has beaten defending champion deity Razor Knuckleface in a cage fight to decide who is to be the next chairman and ruling deity of God Inc. Although superior in size, martial arts prowess, brute strength and unencumbered by brain cells, Knuckleface was defeated by Leroy Cakes's impassioned conviction speech and surrendered his position as Aspirational Concept 35 in favour of his holiness Cakes, who then hired him as a bodyguard. The inauguration ceremony confirming Mr Cakes as Aspirational Concept 36 will take place shortly."

"Captain's Log. 2390.8.26. We are still orbiting space station Lugubrious. Repairs to damage caused by the incompetence and petty vindictiveness of our XO are still underway. However, if we are to meet our secret rendezvous on time while keeping it a secret, we must risk engaging our wormhole generators. My initial high hopes for this mission have been somewhat dampened. This commission is not going to be easy as the crew seem incredibly lazy and thick. Also, I have been feeling unusually moist in the lower area, which I think may have something to do with the imitation plastic material from which the captain's chair is made."

"Captain," Jones's voice interrupted Daisy's recording.

"Yes, XO what is it?"

"Engineering would like to speak with you. Also, and I don't wish to appear incompetent or vindictive, but I would like to suggest to the Captain that if she is going to record a personal log, maybe she shouldn't do it in the middle of the bridge where everyone can hear her."

Daisy looked up. The bridge crew were glaring at her. Ah. Bollocks. She'd got carried away.

"Assuming engines are repaired and we leave now," said Steve, "with a fully extended wormhole and Ion drive at maximum, we should meet our secret rendezvous in an hour. Not that I know anything about a secret rendezvous, what with my being incredibly lazy and thick and it being a secret and all."

"Jeebuzz," muttered Tongue.

"Something to say, Science Officer?"

Tongue realised he'd been overheard but decided to ignore it. "I've checked the engineering status. Much as I hate to say it, I'd recommend further simulation before we engage those engines. A slight delay is acceptable if it means we get there in one piece."

"Tongue, delay is not acceptable. We will reach our —" Daisy looked around uneasily at the bridge officers. Screw it, the cat was already out of the bag and squatting in the litter tray. "We will reach our rendezvous on time." She stabbed at the comms button on the arm of her chair.

"Engineering, prepare for engineering stuff."

"Nau?" came a voice over the intercom.

"Yes, now."

"What do you mean 'yes Nau?', you called me?"

"What?"

"What?"

Jones looked over at Tongue, who had started to gently hit his head on his console.

"Captain," said Jones, "you're speaking to Chief Engineer Nau."

"Yes, thank you for the mansplaining XO, I know who I'm speaking to, which is more than can be said of your grasp of grammatical structure, 'you speaking to chief engineer now', 'me captain and know who me speak to'."

Jones took a deep breath. "You are speaking to Chief Engineer Eric Nau. Nau. N. A. U. The pronunciation of which sounds remarkably like 'now'. Mr Nau is speaking to you. The person to whom you are now speaking is Chief Engineer Eric Nau, AKA Chief Engineer Nau."

"Captain, love a chat and all but did you want something 'cos it's mental down here."

"Yes Mr *Nau*," Daisy glowered at Jones, "I want engines online and ready to leave . . . now."

"Yes?"

Daisy massaged the bridge of her nose. "Chief Engineer, we need to leave orbit . . . immediately. What is your status?"

"Leave orbit?" The chief sucked his teeth. "Well, we've managed to scrape cargo bay one off the engineering pod and auto-docked it with the hull. Because of course only a total mug would try to dock a cargo bay manually."

"Yes, thank you Nau. Carry on . . . Nau."

"There's some minor damage to the hull. The effluent discharge orifices are mangled, we'll need to fix them before we reach Yerboots. I can get the wormhole generators online but the thermo regulators are playing up."

"Could we jerry rig a bypass of the thermo regulators without blowing ourselves up?"

"We could jerry rig a bypass of the thermo regulators without blowing ourselves up but there's another problem."

"Go on?"

"We can't jerry rig a bypass of the thermo regulators without blowing ourselves up."

"I see. What about the Ion drive?"

"Oh bugger, hang on," the comms went silent. After a moment Nau's voice returned. "Sorry Captain, just remembered I left the Ion on."

"Can we get full speed out of it?"

Nau sucked his teeth. "That would mean putting the steamer on."

"Fine. Do it. How long until the wormhole generator is repaired?"

Chief Engineer Nau sucked his teeth again. "Ooh, job like this . . . six years."

"You have 30 mins."

"Thirty minutes? Workmanship of this quality? I'll have to go and get some parts, shouldn't take too long, say three weeks and then I'll only come back after your repeated attempts to contact me fail and then you threaten to go on some media.show about dodgy tradesmen."

"Not three weeks Nau —"

"Now? Leave it out guv!"

"Let me finish — not three weeks Mr Nau, I want it done in thirty minutes."

"Alright, a month, not a second less."

"Thirty minutes."

"OK, fine, thirty minutes."

"You have ten minutes."

"What? Ten minutes? Workmanship of this quality? My dear old mother would die of shame of she wasn't dead already. OK, fine – ten minutes."

"You have five minutes."

"Five minutes? Workmanship of —"

"You have one minute."

"Daisy, Daisy," Jones cut in, "look sorry to interrupt but at some point, you have to stop the demanding captain trope and accept the estimate."

"Done," said Nau.

"Right, let me know when repairs are complete."

"I just said. They're done," Nau repeated. "Finished ten minutes ago. Lovely job."

"You can't have done."

"Yeah, I used my time machine, slipped back and repaired the engines before the accident."

"Time machine?"

"Only a small one. It gets boring down here when we're not in flight, so I thought I'd get myself a hobby."

"Chief," said Tongue, "Time travel is impossible. Or at best incredibly difficult. You can't have solved the equations in your spare moments between shifts."

"It's easy. Look, if you take the basic concepts of symbolic logic and completely ignore them, you get symbolic bollocks and if you get the transformational equations in the right transitional sets, bish bash bosh, whatever way you look at it, the sum of the integers must equal total bollocks, which means you can convert symbolic bollocks into actual bollocks, or, in this case, a time machine."

"That makes no sense," said Daisy, glancing around the bridge for confirmation, "And on the off-chance that it does, you can't repair the engines before they were damaged. That's a paradox or stupid or something."

"Well, only if you think of time as having a single dimension, which it doesn't, actually it has —" A soul-rending scream interrupted the engineer's explanation.

"Jeebuzz, what's happened?!"

"Sorry, that's Mr Kettlewick."

"Who?"

"Mr Kettlewick. Like a total spanner I forgot to adjust the spatial coordinates when I calibrated the time field. Accidentally scooped up Mr Kettlewick from Victorian England and —" the chief was again interrupted by another terrified scream. "Hang on Cap."

The bridge listened as the chief tried to calm his new passenger.

"Kettlewick, again, you are in the future mate. It's the year twenty-three ninety. Science and stuff are all different and stuff. We've gone out into the galaxy and met new life forms, aliens. Sit down and have a cup of splash. It's a lot to take in."

"What in Hades is that! Is this monstrosity one of the hideous things you so calmly refer to as 'aliens', sir?"

"That's a woman Mr Kettlewick."

"A woman Mr Kettlewick? A female doppel-gänger of myself? Can it be?"

"No, I mean 'it's a woman, Mr Kettlewick'."

"There, sir! There, you see the importance of correct grammar and proper deployment of the comma! It was for this very purpose I formed the Society for Appropriately Clenched Grammarians. The membership of said society would venture forth on to the nobles each Sunday, the commons not being a fit place for such esteemed gentlemen, to practise the honourable fighting art of punch-uation in order that we might seek out misusers of the Queen's punctuation and punch them. Thus."

"Ow!"

"Now sir, kindly inform me as to how this hideous thing could possibly be a woman?"

"Well, she is. Assistant Engineer Tamsin Boucher."

"Are you blind sir? It's wearing trousers! Have

you lost possession of your wits? And 'Assistant engineer'? Fie, sir, fie I say! I confess I do not understand what passes for humour in this century of yours. I demand to see the captain!"

"Er, yeah, maybe we should wait till you've had a chance to settle in. The captain's a bit busy right now."

"Busy? Of course, he is. 'Busy' is the correct occupation for such a man. Probably promenading the decks in his finest trousers. Very well, I shall seek an audience at his earliest convenience. For now, I shall inspect these engines of yours."

"You do that Mr Kettlewick. Captain?"

Daisy stopped massaging the bridge of her nose. "So," she said, "Are we ready to leave now, Nau?"

"We need more simulation time."

"Now now Nau, you can do this. We must leave now Nau. Bridge out."

"Captain," said Tongue, "we can afford to delay a few hours."

"Mr Tongue, I will not —" Daisy stopped as she swiveled her chair to face him. "When did you get time to put your hair in plaits and where did that fringe come from?"

He smiled. "Oh this?" he said in a dismissive tone. Daisy's eyes narrowed. She knew that tone. It was a tone that tried to give the impression of a devil-may-care attitude that only someone who has put in hours of work and attention to detail could manage. Dismissive but with a subtle undertone of triumph because someone had noticed. "Our hair automatically adjusts to look great, no matter what the circumstances. I think this is the 'looking professional and in control and yet very cute and potentially available' style. It's nothing, really." He tossed his head casually, just to underline how much of a nothing it wasn't.

"Jeebuzz, I'm glad you're a bloke," muttered Daisy. "Anyway," she continued aloud, "I will not countenance a delay."

She swiveled her chair back to face front, "Mr Power, activate wormhole generators. Set Ion drive to full steam."

"Full steam ahead, aye. Wormhole generators on. Exotic matter projectors active. Wormhole opening."

Daisy leaned forward. Nothing happened. "Steve, what's happening? Or rather, why are things not happening?"

Steve turned to face her. "Oh, sorry Captain, I was waiting for the catchphrase."

"Catchphrase?"

"You know, that pseudo-momentous thing all

captains feel compelled to say when they mean 'go' . . . 'Engage', 'Make it so', 'Get it done', 'One small step', that kind of bollocks."

Daisy suddenly felt uncomfortable as all eyes on the bridge fixed on her. Momentous. OK. Her mind went blank. She looked questioningly at Jones. He just smiled and raised his eyebrows. Bastard. "Er, OK" she said after what seemed like an ice-age. She shuffled forward in her chair and straightened her back. She cleared her throat. "Off we pop!"

The bridge crew visibly deflated. "Right," said Steve, "Off . . . we pop". He pressed a big green button with the word 'Go' crudely written above it in felt tip pen.

The ship shuddered violently and the main bridge lights switched off, leaving the crew illuminated only by the red glow of the emergency lighting.

"Steve, what's happening?" shouted Daisy above the clamour of the . . . well, whatever it was that was clamouring. It sounded like engines trying to heave something way too heavy for them. And stressed metal. There was a lot of stressed metal.

"Nothing to worry about Captain," Steve called back as he held desperately on to the navigation console, "This is perfectly normal." Steve looked toward the main viewer at the front of the bridge. "That, on the other hand, is not."

Daisy followed Steve's gaze. Standing before the main viewer were two anachronistic figures dressed in old-style black tie attire: black bow ties and long-tailed jackets with white gloves. They looked every inch like old-time stage magicians. Except for the inches above their necks. Those inches were very wrong. Instead of human heads, they had what looked like oversized carnival papier mâché heads with garishly painted eyes and cheeks and noses. The figure on the left sported a mouth painted into a happy grin, the sort of happy grin a serial killer might wear while going about her stabby business. The mouth of the figure on the right had been painted into a large, surprised 'O'. Both sported cheeky chappy pencil thin moustaches.

The violent shaking and clamour stopped, and the bridge crew watched the new arrivals in stunned silence.

The pair waved their arms about in a flamboyant 'ta-dah' type flourish, as if their sudden appearance was completely normal and expected.

"Fine," said Jones, "OK, clearly I ate some odd mushroom-type things before coming on duty and this weird stuff is definitely not happening. Agreed?"

"Not unless I ate the same mushrooms, which I didn't. Which means this weird stuff is definitely happening," said Tongue.

Jones glanced over. "Your hair looks fantastic by the way." Alert to the sudden change of circumstance and potential threat, the science officer's hair had once more reconfigured itself, this time into a fetching new hairstyle featuring a cute ponytail.

"Oh, thanks," Tongue smiled back.

The magicians each raised a white-gloved finger to their painted lips in the universally polite gesture that indicated 'shut up'.

Daisy opened her mouth to speak but the words refused to come. Heart pounding, she tried to stand but found herself frozen in place. A glance at the rest of the crew confirmed they were likewise inhibited.

With a now silent audience, the magicians began their performance. The grinning one on the left, which Daisy had unconsciously labelled 'serial killer', raised his hand and inserted a large, rusty key into his right ear. He turned the key several times, each turn eliciting a wince inducing sound, like fingernails scratching against a chalkboard. At the final turn his face swiveled open to reveal a hollow interior containing a violin and bow. These he withdrew and began to play a jaunty tune.

The magician on the right raised his arms to the sides. As his companion began to play, a second head extruded from the top of his head. This was slightly smaller than the original but looked exactly the same in all other respects, down to the 'O' shape of the mouth. A third head extruded from the second and then a fourth and a fifth.

The extra heads leapt down, and the magician juggled them expertly in his hands, each head emitting a warbling falsetto song as he did so.

Daisy couldn't be sure, but she was fairly certain that none of this was even remotely alluded to in the captain's course prospectus.

When serial killer finished his ditty, he neatly replaced his violin in his head, closed his face and removed the key from his ear. His companion threw his extra heads into the air. His oval mouth opened even wider and he swallowed each of them as they descended.

The magicians repeated their 'ta-dah' gesture and the bridge crew erupted into spontaneous and involuntary applause.

The lights went out.

When they came on again, the crew found themselves seated in a barber's shop. OK, weird, thought

Daisy. But relatable at least. The fact that they were all having their hair enthusiastically cut by a very bushy plant, wielding scissors at the ends of its various branches and shoots, was somewhat less relatable. Daisy sniffed at the pungent aroma in the air.

"Relax, it's a cannabis plant," said Jones, glancing over at her. He leaned over conspiratorially "I think it's stoned," he said, sotto voce.

"Oh well, that's alright then," replied Daisy, flinching as two pairs of scissors snipped dangerously close to her eyes.

From the corner of the room, a crackling song issued from the horn of an old gramophone, its speed alternating slow and fast in time with the speed at which a grinning white-gloved gentleman turned the crank handle.

Steve screamed and writhed as the plant cut what remained of his wispy, long hair.

Daisy glanced across at Tongue, whose hair was putting up a brave fight with the plant, utilising what appeared to be a hair based version of Wing Chun. The plant seemed somewhat nonplussed, as if it was not entirely used to hair reacting this way. Which, to be fair, could be said of Tongue's hair and hairdressing plants.

"What the hell are you grinning at?" Daisy demanded of Jones.

"Oh, nothing," he said, "Just enjoying the effects of exotic particles from an unstable wormhole bouncing off our collective subconscious and fracturing reality. Let me know when you want me to fix it."

"If you know how to fix it, fix it!" shouted Tongue.

"I'm afraid that order would have to come directly from the Captain."

"It'll be a cold day in hell before I ask for your help!" hissed Daisy.

"Fine. In the meantime, I'm long overdue a haircut."

The vines abruptly stopped snipping and lowered their scissors to the jugular vein of each crew member. Flesh dimpled as the points of the scissors pressed in.

"How you doing for throat cuts?" said Daisy.

"Would this be your subconscious making some sort of point?" Jones's confidence of a moment ago had fled. He remained very still as he watched the scissors at his throat in the mirror.

"I don't know XO. But in case you hadn't noticed,

my subconscious hasn't excluded me from the lesson."

"Yeah, you're right, screw this," he said, "OK Mic, full stop. Cut engines."

Immediately, they were back on Space Scrap 17. Daisy urgently scanned the bridge. Everything was back to normal. Except Tongue. His hair was a Medusa-style explosion of outrage.

Mic Vol stood next to the navigation console, his hand firmly pressed on the big red button labelled 'Stop'.

"Well done, Mic," breathed Jones.

Tongue slammed his fist down on his console. "You two," he glared at Jones and Daisy, "My cabin. Now." He span on his heel then stopped. "And if ANYONE mentions my hair, my breasts will pump venom into my death quills."

Tongue balled his fists and stomped from the bridge.

"I don't know about anyone else," said Steve into the subsequent silence, "But I'd quite like to see that."

Daisy and Jones looked at each other.

Jones shrugged. "Bad hair day?"

UPON ARRIVAL AT HIS CABIN, Tongue had been greeted with several covert messages. None of them were particularly welcome. Politically, the Galactic situation had worsened in the last few hours and events were moving at an alarming rate. He took a deep, steadying breath.

The intercom buzzed. Oh great, he thought. Tweedledum and Tweedledee. "Come," he said.

The door opened, admitting the captain and XO.

"My door doesn't do that, does your door do that?" said Jones, watching the door glide smoothly shut again.

"What, open and close?" said Daisy, "No, not without protest and a lot of kicking and swearing."

"That's what I thought. You, how come you get the only functioning door on the ship — JEEBUZZ!"

Jones and Daisy took an involuntary step back, eyes wide and teeth bared in a terrified rictus.

This was not the sort of reaction Tongue was used to. Awe, yes. Declarations of love, yes. Sometimes people would stop and compose sonnets to his beauty on the spot and declare undying love. Or swear that they would henceforth become hermits, foregoing all contact with other people because they had already seen the epitome of beauty and everything else was liable to be a massive disappointment. Indeed, Tongue had received begging letters from mental health specialists asking him to tone it down, since one look at him and their patients knew that the rest of their lives were going to be pale and shallow by comparison. He had also received begging letters from pharmaceutical companies asking if he could possibly ramp it up a bit because wherever he went, sales of antidepressants went through the roof. Mostly, though, people just dribbled.

These reactions he was used to. Fear and shock, he was not.

Frowning, he went into the bathroom and looked in the mirror.

He screamed.

He emerged from the bathroom ten minutes

later.

"My apologies, Captain, XO. I'm afraid events of the last half hour have confused my hair. Our recent experiences have been somewhat novel, and my hair had no idea how to compose itself. It tried to adopt several different styles and colours at the same time. The outcome was . . . regrettable."

"Regrettable? It was hair-ageddon!" said Jones.

"Shut up Jones," said Daisy.

"No, he's right. On my way here from the bridge I passed several crew members who either screamed and ran away or fainted on the spot. Damn it," a sudden wave of emotion swept over Tongue, "I have enough pressures already, why must I be gorgeous no matter what the circumstances?"

"Tongue, don't give it a second thought," said Daisy. "Your hair looks lovely now. All those . . . tight cascading curls and the way it shines. It's just not right the way society puts pressure on people like us."

"You seem able to resist it without any problems," said Jones.

Daisy gave him a flat stare.

"Society?" said Tongue. "What do you mean? Society doesn't pressure me and even if it made the attempt, like any rational being capable of independent thought I would simply ignore it."

Daisy frowned, confused. "Sorry, I thought you were upset at having to constantly look gorgeous. It's nothing to be ashamed of, we all feel that way from time to time."

"Yeah, the sleepless nights I endure, worrying about having to be gorgeous all the time," said Jones.

"Shut up unless you want to clean the toilets for the next month."

"I was upset. Temporarily," said Tongue. "But that's got nothing to do with 'society'. Like individuals in all species I'm driven by my own evolutionary psychology, which motivates me, in essence, to adopt whatever behaviours it thinks will allow me to successfully reproduce. In other words, if I'm feeling any pressure it is only the pressure that I place upon myself. Any other conclusion would be a pathetic attempt to abdicate responsibility for one's own actions. Why would anyone do that, it's vacuous. Not to mention neurotic."

"Sorry, I was just expressing what we humans call an emotion, the emotion of 'empathy'," said Daisy.

"And now she's expressing the human emotion of 'Patronising bitch' along with another old favourite, 'talking bollocks'. Got any drink? I need a drink."

"You see why I left him," said Daisy.

"You didn't leave me, I left you. My letter was on the kitchen table first."

"ENOUGH!" Tongue's death quills erupted from his fists. He couldn't help it. Events had taken their toll on his patience and he was in no mood for more bickering between these two idiots.

Daisy and Jones stood transfixed.

"Enough," repeated Tongue, retracting his death quills with an effort. "Now, I don't know what it is between you two, BUT," he said as they both opened their mouths to begin another round of accusations, "It ends here. Your stupid, petty little squabble has put this mission in danger. Do you realise what is at stake here? Do you?"

Daisy and Jones stared at their feet, which were shuffling uncomfortably.

"Have you seen the news?"

They shook their heads.

Tongue stabbed at a button. The monitor sprang into life.

"Oh Jeebuzz, I hate newscasts. If you want me to watch this, I definitely need a drink," complained Jones.

"Shut up and watch. This went out in the last half hour."

The monitor showed a newscast interview

featuring a hard-nosed, sneering newsbot seated across from a smartly dressed businessman.

"Welcome back morons" sneered the Paxbot. "I have with me Sir Reginald Ponce, archbishop of God Inc."

"Good evening Mr Paxbot, pleasure to be here."

"Oh, shut up. So, Sir Reginald, we have a new aspirational concept — bit of a ham-fisted cock-up on your part?"

The archbishop shook his head. "Not at all, myself and the rest of the board are very excited."

Paxbot's face screwed up in distaste as if he were chewing a wasp that he had expected to taste of delicious chocolate but instead turned out to taste of angry wasp and canine genitals. "Oh come on, Leroy Cakes has stated he will be a conviction god and not a career god. As such he is clearly not the candidate favoured by the board of God Inc. In fact, if it were not for his surprise win in the cage fight, your chairman would still be Razor Knuckleface."

Sir Reginald made the requisite PR media course approved mollifying gestures. "The wishes of the board do not enter into it. As you know Paxbot, the chairman of God Inc, God himself as acting Aspirational Concept to the galaxy, is selected by a fight to the death in the cage. That is democracy."

"But it wasn't a fight to the death was it? Razor Knuckleface is still alive and has, in point of fact, been appointed Mr Cakes's personal bodyguard. And keep your hands still or I will cut off your arms, you self-serving, duplicitous twat."

Sir Reginald smiled, was about to raise his arms in 'Mollifying Gesture #12' but decided against. "Under theocratic rules," he said instead, sitting on his hands, "the death does not have to be a physical one. Some would say, myself among them, that not all the sacred rules of the cage fight are intended to be interpreted literally. Some of them are intended to be viewed as allegorical or metaphorical. 'No underpants to be worn on the head within the cage' is obviously literal. But the holy writ of all Aspirational Concepts since the formation of God Inc has been that there is an afterlife. And since the soul is eternal, the concept of death is itself a nonsense. We must, in this sense, infer a metaphorical intent."

"Like the vexed question of how many angels can dance of the head of a pin?"

"No. That is perfectly literal, the answer is three. You have clearly not read my white paper 'Pinheads are only wide enough to accommodate three angels – the campaign for wider pinheads'."

"Patronise me again, you money-grubbing flap

sucker, and I will eviscerate you. The point is that as a conviction god and therefore possessing moral values, Mr Cakes was always going to be a controversial candidate. And don't deny that or I will cut off your face with a velvet spoon."

"Let's make no mistake here Paxbot — mistakes are wrong, and should be avoided at all costs, unless the costs mistakenly account for them — in which case, mistakes are right. Or at least accounted for. That is democracy."

A low growl issued from the Paxbot's throat. "But the board of Miasma Inc have been outspoken in their criticism of Mr Cakes. And since Miasma owns God Inc, surely their views represent the real position?"

"The views of Miasma Inc are not for the likes of you or I to question. It is a private company and as such a law unto itself. They are accountable to no one, not you or I and certainly not the public at large. They are, if you like, tyrants. That is democracy."

Paxbot sat glaring at the archbishop for a moment. "Right, I've had enough of this," he said, knives springing from his mechanical fists, "I'm going to cut off your ears because you're clearly not listening and —" he paused, hand held up to his ear. The fact that he had now inadvertently stabbed himself in the face with his fist knife did not seem to faze him. "Wait, I'm hearing from the gallery that . . . yes, we have an insta link with His Holiness. Leroy Cakes himself has called the studio and would like to contribute to the discussion."

Sir Reginald almost leapt from his chair. "Wait, what? As archbishop I condemn this as heresy."

"But Leroy Cakes is now god. How can god's word be heresy?"

". . . As archbishop I condemn this as hearsay."

A screen insert appeared between them. It showed a live feed of Leroy Cakes. He had a kindly, rumpled face with a straggly white beard. Not the sort of visage one would normally associate with the mindless thugs that usually occupied the position of god. More the visage of a kindly uncle, and not even one of the ones your parents warn you to stay away from.

"Your Holiness, thank you for joining us."

"It is my pleasure, Paxbot. Please, do not avert your eyes."

"Thank you, Oh Super One. But I would ask, if I may, to what do we owe the pleasure of your attendance?"

Aspirational Concepts, even those that had not

yet been inaugurated, seldom spoke to anyone outside the board of God Inc.

"The archbishop makes several good points and, once inaugurated, I shall certainly be backing his campaign for wider pinheads and I would like to say that I forgive all the outrageous lies, slander and libels aimed at me by the boards of both Miasma and God Inc."

"Praise be," said a clearly relieved Sir Reginald.

"I forgive them because their comments are trite and meaningless. The galaxy has been freed from Miasma's grip on the food supply. Since my invention of pseudo food, each person can now reconstitute food from their own faecal matter."

"Holy shit," muttered Sir Reginald.

"Yes, you are," sneered Paxbot.

"However, this invention has hit their profit margins and they intend to compensate for their losses by incitement of galactic war, thereby increasing the profits of the arm of their company devoted to arms manufacture."

"The arms manufacture arm?"

"Yes. Pseudo food has cost them an arm and a leg. And they won't stand for it."

"All private companies are ordained to obey the holy profits!" protested Sir Reginald.

"One more word," said Paxbot, raising a threatening fist knife.

"Once inaugurated," continued Cakes, "I shall have access to all records necessary to proving my case. I shall not rest until all the board members of Miasma and God Inc are behind bars."

"Outrageous —" which was as far as Sir Reginald got before Paxbot's knife slammed into his left eye.

Tongue switched off the screen.

"It all gets a bit messy after that. But the important point is this — it is imperative that these talks go ahead. If the Ululations join the Loose Association, then Leroy Cakes stands a better chance of winning the doves around, thus preventing a destructive and needless war. We need to make that rendezvous with the LASS Square Jaw."

"That's all very well," said Jones, "but the engines are screwed, the cargo bay sewage discharge orifices are mangled, the —"

"I have spoken with Engineer Nau. We can print enough Blokes to assist with the work. If we focus on the essential engine repairs, we can be under way in just over an hour."

Daisy scanned the DEVICE Tongue handed her. "But that would take all our remaining pseudo carbon blocks!"

Tongue pursed his lips. "Were you listening to the stuff about the war and the doves and things?"

"Fine," said Daisy returning the DEVICE.

"And in the meantime, Captain, XO, you need to put your differences aside. At least until we reach the rendezvous. After that, I don't care what you do. Understood?"

"Of course. Even though this is all Jones's fault."

"My fault! What about —"

The sound of Tongue's newly extruded death quills tapping on his DEVICE brought their recriminations to a sudden halt.

They exchanged quick, nervous glances. "Yes Ambassador, you've made your position quite clear," said Daisy quickly.

For a few minutes Tongue stared after their retreating backs. Leroy Cakes's ill-advised declaration was going to annoy a lot of people. Especially Tongue's secret employers. Despite what he claimed publicly, Tongue's orders were to ensure that the talks did not take place. But to do that, he first had to get to the LASS Square Jaw. Which meant the success of his mission, or at least part of it, was dependent on idiots.

ONE HOUR and twenty minutes later, the bridge crew were once more assembled.

"Repairs complete, simulations check out," the chief engineer's voice came over the intercom, "In fact I've been able to complete some outstanding maintenance on the Ion drive."

"No need to brag, Chief," said Daisy.

"By outstanding, I mean 'long overdue'. But now that you mention it the results *are* a bit tasty. We should be able to hit Mark 7, with a cruising speed of Mark 5."

"Blimey," said Steve, "We don't usually make more than Mark 3 and that's if we get out and push."

"Well done, prepare to engage wormhole, bridge out."

"I have no need to remind the Captain that it is

usually at this point," said Jones from the XO station, "that the Captain should request a final status before setting off. You know, a brief summary of things and stuff."

An hour ago, Daisy would have bristled at Jones's intervention, regarded it as yet another attempt to undermine her authority. But after Tongue's tongue-lashing it had occurred to her that Jones could easily have exposed her cheating at the exams. That she had cheated was something of a scandal. That she had done so using a temporary and illegal mind patch was even more so. That she had done so using an illegal mind patch of the most notorious pirate captain in human space history, the ravenous xeno-phobe Captain Weaver, elevated her 'something of a scandal' to the 'epitome of scandal', the very defini-tion of 'a right shocker and no mistake'. But Jones had kept his mouth shut. She was grateful and she told him so on their way back to the bridge. She had also suggested that they should put aside their history and work together — at least for the duration of this mission. Jones had stopped walking.

"Yeah, look, it was just a bit of a shock, you know, seeing you and what happened and stuff. It all got complicated and annoying."

"Yes. I suppose it put us both on our guard."

Jones laughed then, "Letters? I mean what kind of a coward ends a relationship with a letter? Jeebuzz, we're terrible people aren't we."

Daisy agreed. "So, pax then?"

He smiled. "Yes, go on. Let's see where it goes. We might work well together."

"Yes," she enthusiastically agreed, caught up in the sudden mood of bonhomie, "We might end up fuck buddies!"

They both stared at each other in shocked silence. "Well, uh," said Jones, "I think the bridge is this way."

"No, that's the toilet," pointed out Daisy, "It's this way."

"Right, yes, lead on Captain."

Since then, the atmosphere on the bridge had been far less prickly.

"Thank you, XO," replied Daisy, "As you say, you have no need to tell me that it is usually at this point that the captain would . . . erm . . ."

"Request a status . . ."

"Request a final status before setting off, yes, that. Final status XO?"

"Wormhole generators showing green —"

"Oh, bloody hell, engineering just said the repairs are complete. Now this?"

"No," said Jones gently, "That's good. Green is good. Puce is worrying."

"Oh, right, I knew that. Carry on."

"So, wormhole generators good, Ion set to full steam, course laid in. All systems look ready for the Captain's pleasure."

"Filthy systems."

"No, I mean —"

"I know what you mean XO. Your captain was making a joke," she turned in her chair to smile at him.

"Oh," said Steve, "Shall I add that to the official log?"

"No. What?" she turned back to face front.

"It's just Captain Trevor used to like us to make a note of it when he made a joke. He'd make us read them back every month."

"No, Steve, that won't be necessary. Right, activate exotic matter, Ion drive to Mark 1. Bring the wormhole online."

The main viewer showed the customary pyrotechnic display that resulted from energetic exotic matter particles being projected at a single point in space-time, making the ordinary space around it recoil in a horrified scream that was a scrambled mix of hard, soft and lightly poached radiation, all of which resulted in a spaceship-sized hole through to hyperspace.

"Wormhole open."

"Thank you, Navigation Officer. Right, off we pop."

"Popping off . . . now." Steve hit the big, green button.

In a flash, the mouth of the wormhole grew larger on the main viewer and then all was darkness as Space Scrap 17 shot through the entry into hyperspace and sped toward its destination.

"We are at Mark 1. All systems look good."

"OK, let's take it to Mark 4. That should bring us to our rendezvous in . . ." Daisy's brow furrowed as she attempted to calculate their arrival time. "In time to do the rendezvous thing," she finished.

"Mark 4, aye."

Two hours later a similar pyrotechnic display in another sector of deep space heralded the opening of a wormhole exit point. Space Scrap 17 exited the wormhole and returned to normal space-time.

Empty, normal space-time.

Empty that is, aside from the mountain-sized pieces of rock floating around.

But very conspicuously empty of the flag-ship of the LASS space fleet, the heavily armoured and bristling with weapons-grade weapons, LASS Square Jaw.

Of which there was no trace.

#

"Something's wrong," said Tongue. He ran the sensor scans again, this time extending the range to maximum. He frowned. "Captain, there is no sign of the Square Jaw."

"Oh good."

"Good?"

"Well, they won't notice we were late." Daisy raised her thumbs and grinned.

Tongue inclined his head. "You wish to join me in performing double penetration?"

"What? No, I mean 'good'. You know, thumbs up, the universal gesture of approval. Isn't that . . . isn't that what it means on your world?"

"Er, no. Unless the recipient of the gesture is in favour, in which case I suppose it could be considered a gesture of approval. Sort of . . ."

"That's the problem with universal gestures. No consistency," said Jones. "But the bigger problem is — where is the Square Jaw?"

Tongue shook himself. "Mic, anything on communication channels? Set to widest bandwidth."

Mic Vol bent to his console. "No. Nothing. Some unusually heavy radiation static though."

"Captain," called Steve, "I don't know where we are. I'm running the standard navigation sweeps and . . ."

"And?" said Daisy, impatiently.

"And we should have exited fairly close to Jagrapax II. A super Earth. But it's not here. There should be four planets in this system, but I can't find any of them. Nothing but those huge rocks."

Jones swallowed, his mouth suddenly dry. "Steve, could those . . . could those huge, actually very huge, massive in fact, pieces of rock also be accurately described as pieces of . . . well not to put too fine a point on it, could they be described as pieces of planet?"

"Well, I mean, yes, I suppose, they are big enough."

Jones bit his upper lip. "Hmm. Steve, just out of interest, are there similar collections of huge rocks at the locations where the other planets in the system should be?"

"Er," Steve consulted his board, "Yes! Yes, there

are! Ah, no, except where the fourth planet should be. That's a gas giant."

"Oh, good. So that's there is it?"

"No. Just massive chunks of ice."

"Shit," muttered Jones, "Massive chunks of ice resembling what one would expect if a gas giant had been, say, I dunno, super cooled into a massive ball of ice and then smashed to flaps?"

Steve laughed, "Do you know, they could." He shrugged and shook his head. "I just don't know what to make of it all. We must be in the wrong place."

"Oh, we are definitely in the wrong place," said Jones emphatically. "Daisy, we need to get out of here right now."

Daisy twisted in her seat. "Explain?"

"Explain? Four planets have been taken apart and we don't want to meet whoever did it."

"Jones, no one can take apart a planet. Stop being such a namby. We have to wait for the Square Jaw. They can't waggle their fingers and cluck about our timekeeping now. If anything, I might put in a complaint about them. Flag-ship of the fleet, my arse!"

"I'm getting something on audio," called Mic.

"There you see," said Daisy, "probably apologising for their tardiness. Put it on speaker Mr Vol, let's all enjoy their squirming." Daisy turned back in her seat and crossed her arms.

The speakers crackled and then came an urgent voice, "This is a distress call from the LASS Square Jaw. Message follows: This is the captain of the LASS Square Jaw. Argh! Help! Jeebuzz look at the size of that bastard! What the frigging flaps is it?! Run, help, argh! Mummy!" There came the sound of an explosion and the message fell silent.

The bridge crew sat and stood in stunned silence.

Steve shook his head and shrugged, "Well I'm flummoxed. What can it all mean?"

"XO," said Daisy, "I have reconsidered your former proposal and on further consideration find myself in complete agreement with your assessment. Steve, get us the hell out of here! Now!"

"Wait," Tongue held up his hand. "Captain, I'm detecting an Ion engine trace leading out of this system."

"The Square Jaw . . . or huge, planet-killing bastard?" asked Daisy.

"Square Jaw. The trace matches their engine signature. They must have burned the engines pretty hard. Feeding coordinates to helm."

"If it leads away from here that's fine by me.

Steve, lay in a course to pursue the Square Jaw. Mark 7. Pop."

Steve laid in the course and smashed his fist down on the 'Go' button.

Space Scrap 17's Ion engines burst into life and the ship flashed away from what remained of the Jagrapax system.

ION ENGINE TRAILS are pretty much indistinguishable from one another. But a few centuries ago, it had become fashionable for young, rich owners of hot-rod spaceships to modify the Coulomb field manipulators of their engines to write the name of their ship, along with an insulting note, in the Xenon gas trail left in the wake of their vessels.

This fashion was quickly superseded by a newer and rather more violent fashion, whereby the people offended by the insulting note followed the trail of the hot-rods, located their owners, and beat the living crap out of them.

However, the idea of making all spacecraft Ion trails contain a unique identifier was seized upon and made a legal requirement by the Loose Association space fleet. It was an easy way to identify spacecraft owners, particularly the ones who had fallen behind on their regular service schedule.

"Ion trail thinning," said Tongue from his station. "Looks like they stopped here."

"OK Steve, engines off. Mic, any communications traffic?"

"Nothing Captain. But that spike in radiation static has returned."

"As have the big chunks of rock that look suspiciously like chewed up planets," said Jones. "Steve, assuming our last location was the Jagrapax system, where are we now?"

Steve did some quick calculations, "Er, well, according to this we should be in the Cuk system. Seven planets. Three uninhabitable, four heavily populated."

"And where there should be planets?"

"Nothing. Nothing but these floating piles of rubble. You know what this means?"

"Yes?" said Jones patiently.

"This means someone must have created a device capable of cloaking entire planets."

Jones ran his hands over his face. "And the rubble?"

"Ah well," said Steve now eagerly into his

conspiracy, "That was just to throw us off the scent. Cunning bastards."

"Yes, Steve it could mean that — or it could mean a planet-busting bastard has reduced these planets to rubble just like it did at Jagrapax."

Steve just gaped at him, eyes wide. He emitted a strangled tension chuckle.

"Captain, I've found the Square Jaw," said Tongue. "In the vicinity of the second planet. Or what remains of the second planet."

"Oh, thank Jeebuzz," said Steve, "She's got weapons and shields and everything. We're saved!"

"Tongue, feed her coordinates to the helm," said Daisy sounding equally relieved, "Steve take us to her, Mic tell her we're coming."

The bridge crew watched the main view screen intently as Space Scrap 17 approached the LASS Square Jaw,

"There!" shouted Jones pointing to the viewer. In the distance was a bright dot, small but definitely the profile of a space fleet multi-mission starship.

"Mic, any response from them yet?"

"None Captain. But the background radiation may be scattering the signal."

"Or not," said Jones flatly.

As they approached, it became obvious that the flag-ship of the space fleet was dead in space.

"Hooray," said Steve, "the Square Jaw."

"Yes Steve" said Daisy.

"And it's having a rest, just lying around waiting for us and now we're all safe and — it's dead isn't it."

"Yes Steve," said Daisy.

The Square Jaw hung in space. That it had been in battle was obvious from the myriad black scorch marks that seared across almost every part of its armour plating. Parts of the hull were exposed to space, ripped open by something powerful and unforgiving and relentless.

Daisy sat forward in her seat. "Jeebuzz, what happened here? Life signs Mic?"

"Dead," said Mic.

"What, all of them?"

Mic turned to her. "What?"

"All the crew are dead?"

"The crew?"

"Yes!"

"No, I was talking about comms. All channels are dead."

"Right, so what about life signs?"

"All dead."

"No life signs at all?"

Mic stood, "Ah, you must be the new captain. Welcome aboard, I am Mic Vol your communications officer."

"What are you —" Daisy stopped, suddenly remembering her conversation with Mic when she had first come aboard.

She and Mic both made "Ahhhhh" noises and pointed at each other.

Steve looked alternately at Daisy and Mic as their temporal conversation played itself out. "Sorry, am I the only one not following this?"

"Captain, we need to find out what happened here," said Tongue, leaving his station to stand before her.

"Something nasty," said Jones, "We need to run away. Now, before that thing comes back."

"Why should it come back?" shot Tongue.

"Well, I don't know, maybe it had the Square Jaw for starters, followed by a delicious buffet selection of all the planets in this star system for main course and now it's looking for a Space Scrap 17 shaped cheese board!"

Tongue addressed Daisy again, "We need to find out what happened. This may be related to the peace talks ."

"Ya think?" muttered Jones.

Tongue shot Jones a look that could have done nasty things to metal plating. Jones was fortunate in that he had no metal plates in his head. But just to be on the safe side, he thought it best to pretend to be distracted by something on his console before Tongue's stare also developed bio-weapon capabilities.

Tongue dragged his attention away from Jones and back to the captain. "What if someone were trying to prevent the Ululations reaching Blah-Blah? As Yerbootsian ambassador to the Ululation delegation, I demand we make the effort. Lives are at stake."

"Yeah," said Jones, "Ours," he gulped as he realised he had spoken aloud. "Oh look," he said, pointing at another area on his console, "There's a . . . oooh, better do . . . the thing, hmmm," he frowned down at his console.

"Captain we need to access the logs from the Square Jaw," said Tongue, who had decided to kill Jones at a more opportune time.

"Well, that's easy enough. Mic establish a link to the Square Jaw's computer."

"Yes," said Mic, "That's something I should know how to do. Ummm," he bent to his console and stabbed at a few buttons hopefully.

"No," said Tongue. "Ship's logs and mission briefs

are not available on the open network. We have to go over there."

"Of course we do," said Daisy, pinching the brow of her nose.

"Wait a minute . . ." said Steve.

"You have an idea?"

". . . I thought he was a science officer, what's all this about ambassador?"

"That'll be a 'no' then."

"Don't worry your tiny brain about it, Steve," Jones gave up pretending to do the thing, "Look we can't get over there. The shuttle bay exit is buggered, we haven't had time to repair it."

"Well then it's a spacewalk," said Tongue, "I volunteer."

"Ah, your kind are invulnerable to hard radiation? Good," said Mic.

"No," replied Tongue frowning.

"It's just that the peculiar radiation in this system exceeds the tolerance of our space suits — by the time your body arrived at the Square Jaw, you would be quite dead."

"We have to know what happened here. The fate of the galaxy depends upon it." Tongue's hair had twisted itself into a short, severe style. The sort of haircut you did not argue with.

"I see two main temporal outcomes to this discussion," said Mic.

"You see what?" said Jones.

"It's . . . Mic, his species sees time differently, sort of all at once and in bits," said Daisy. "That conversation we just had. We had it earlier today as well. He was having a conversation in the present and the future. Or something."

"Oh well, that's cleared that up," said Jones.

"Go on Mic, what do you see?"

"Well Captain, these are just impressions you understand but if we go to the Square Jaw and retrieve the information the ambassador requires, things get bad."

"And if we don't," said Jones, "then things go extremely well, and everyone gets ice cream and cake?"

"You're not going to like this."

"Argh"

"If we don't go over there, things get horrifically bad. Very nasty. I am going to have nightmares over what I see of that potential outcome and I am someone who took in his stride the effects on the Marauding Buttocks of Sis after their atmosphere was ravaged by violent laxative storms."

"Right," said Daisy into the resulting stunned

silence. "Well, that leaves no alternative then." She stood. "Jones, Tongue, meet me in the medical bay. Mic tell Doctor Smiert we're on our way."

"Where are you going?" Jones called after her.

"I need to get something from my cabin," Daisy said as she exited the bridge.

SMIERT DISLIKED MOST THINGS. But what she disliked most of all were interruptions. Her medical bay was an island of peace and quiet and, more importantly, a solitary place where she could pursue her work unhindered by the squeamish and those that scream of unethical practice. And those that simply screamed. How she longed for old Mother Russia. Life must have been so simple in the KGB.

Daisy entered the room carrying a small case.

"Captain, I protest. What is meaning of interruption?"

"The meaning of this interruption, Doctor, is that whatever you were previously doing has now been interrupted. Tongue, have you brought the doctor up to speed?"

"Yes."

"He has but I don't see how you get across to other ship by standing in my laboratory — damnit — medical bay."

"With this," said Daisy, placing her case upon the desk.

"And this is what?"

Daisy opened the case, revealing a complex device of dials and tubes and electrodes. Tongue whistled, "Is that what they call the 'retro look'?"

"No," said Daisy, "it's a . . . well, it's a . . ."

"It's a neural uploader," said Jones. "A very illegal neural uploader. So illegal in fact that all the originals were destroyed. If you want one these days, they have to be cobbled together out of the engineering equivalent of flotsam and jetsam just so that the AI's don't spot what you're up to by analysing your supply orders."

"You're suspiciously well informed, Mr Jones," said Daisy.

"Lucky guess," said Jones.

The doctor was making an awed inspection of the Frankenstein device. "And you have this why?"

Daisy knew this question would be coming but still had no good answer. Her mouth opened and shut a few times, but no words were brave enough to leave it.

"Classified," said Jones.

Brilliant! Daisy nodded her approval at Jones's improvisation.

"You could be killed just for knowing about it," he added.

Daisy frowned and shook her head at his unnecessary elaboration.

Jones realised his mistake and began to panic. "I could be killed for telling you that you could be killed for even knowing about it, so forget I said anything about killing . . . or me speaking . . . at all. Ever."

"Anyway," asserted Daisy before Jones could dig his hole any deeper, "we need to get to the Square Jaw to access its private network. Can't use the shuttle craft, space suits are no good, so —"

"So, we all upload our consciousness to the computer and hide from whatever kicked the shit out this star system!"

"No XO," said Daisy wearily, "Tongue, Chief Nau and I will upload our consciousness to the computer and send our digital minds over to the Square Jaw. Then we download ourselves from the Square Jaw's computer into a couple of Blokes. We direct the Blokes to access the private network, learn what we can and transfer ourselves back here.

Doctor, I will need you to supervise the upload and our vitals."

"Excellent!" said Tongue. "If I recall correctly this was a favourite tactic of your Captain Weaver during her pirate years. You must have come top of your class for space history during your captain's exams."

"Er, yes, that," said Daisy.

"Yes, she didn't know that because she downloaded Captain Weavers's mind patch or anything." Jones looked up, realising he had said the words aloud. "That would be ridiculous, ha ha." He blanched as everyone regarded him in silence. "Ridiculous," he added weakly.

Chief Engineer Nau entered the room.

"Oh, thank Jeebuzz!" said Jones.

"Chief, all ready?" said Daisy.

"Yep, all good. I left Mr Kettlewick in charge of engineering."

"Kettlewick? The Victorian?"

"Yeah, well he's stopped screaming now and he was an industrial engineer in 1856. So, our engines make perfect sense to him. Anyway, there ain't anyone else. Oh nice, a neural uploader."

Doctor Smiert wasted no time in preparation for transfer. She assembled the equipment while the others discussed the mission or, as she thought of it, 'stood around being irrelevant'. As she worked, her mind was feverishly trying to figure out how she could steal the neural uploader. Oh, the applications, the applications!

She arranged three gurneys and placed the uploader on a wheeled trolley. She took the cable from one end of the unit and plugged it into the computer. Then, after running through some final tests and tuning with Chief Nau, her preparations were complete.

"My preparations are complete," she said. "Neural upload can only handle one set of brain patterns at time. It will suck out your mind through these," she held up a couple of wires attached to the device, "digitize and transfer to computer. Then send to computer on other ship."

"Alright, Chief Nau first, then me, then Tongue," said Daisy.

"Be aware, only basic brain functions remain. You need to return to your body within two hours or your body die. If your host body die over there, you are turnip brain. Understood?"

"Get back in two hours and don't die, got it, let's get a move on" said Tongue.

"Just sign this please," Smiert handed each of them a DEVICE.

"What's this?" asked Daisy.

"If you die, I get to harvest your bodies," said Smiert.

"For organ donations, that sort of thing?"

"Organ donations? Ha, ha, yes, good one." It took Smiert a second to realise no one else was laughing, "Oh yes! Organ donations, yes, that, medical research not experimentation or . . . food."

"What are you babbling about Smiert? Food for what?"

At that moment a hitherto unnoticed metal door shuddered as something slammed into it. Above the door was a sign reading 'KEEP OUT' and with the words 'BUT NOT THEM — KEEP THEM IN' scrawled in pen underneath.

Smiert shouted something in angry Russian and the thumping stopped. "Um, yes, as I was saying, food for thought. Not . . . food for them. Of course," she said with as much of an air of faux innocence as she could muster.

"What have you got in there?" asked Tongue suspiciously, taking a step toward the door.

"Time is short, yes?" said Smiert, holding up the neural upload head-piece.

"Yes, OK Chief, on you pop," said Daisy, indicating one of the gurneys.

When Nau had made himself comfortable, Smiert placed the helmet on his head.

"Ready?"

"Ready."

"May be very painful," she said. "Very, very painful."

"What? You didn't mention —" but before the chief could finish, Smiert flipped the switch. The engineer's body slumped, and his eyes closed.

"Hmm. Or not," said Smiert, disappointed. She studied the computer terminal. "Da. Upload complete."

Jones crossed the room to the comms panel, "Mic, send the data package over."

Smiert repeated the process with Daisy and Tongue.

"OK," said Jones. "I'll be on the bridge. Keep monitoring their vitals, let me know if there's any change."

"Of course."

"And Doctor," Jones paused by the door, "make sure nothing happens to them. I don't want to have to feed you to whatever that is in there."

Smiert nodded, noting the unusual hardness of his tone. There was promise in that one, she thought.

"Captain, all OK?" Jones's voice sounded over the ship to ship intercom.

"Yes. I think so, er yes," Daisy looked around at her colleagues who paused in their work on the gleaming bridge to nod. "Yes, all OK."

"So, what's it like being in a printed body?"

"It's an odd sensation, sort of like living inside a mushroom."

"Can't say the analogy is working for me."

"Well, imagine what it would be like to have flesh made of mushroom . . . that. The tactile senses are very dull. And breathing is weird. Blokes don't need to breathe but my brain keeps wanting to."

"Right, well keep doing it — you don't want your brain suddenly deciding that breathing is old school and a bit last year. Might make things difficult when you get back to your real body. And don't get comfortable — you've got less than two hours in that body."

"You wouldn't believe this bridge XO. It's all chrome and fitted panels. It's even got carpet on the walls. We should have carpet on the walls. Why don't we have carpet on the walls?"

"Because we're not a management consultancy office in space. It sounds horrible. Any damage?"

"There's a couple of blown panels here and there but less than you'd expect from the state of the hull. And there's a weird sticky liquid on some of the chairs," she dabbed a finger into one of the pools and watched as sticky strands formed between the fingers of her borrowed body's hand. "No crew though. Not even bodies."

"Captain, I've got the logs."

"Sounds nasty," said Jones.

"Shut up XO, captain out." Daisy walked over to where Tongue was examining a panel. It felt like walking in an inflated body suit.

"Right, can we put it on the view screen? Where the hell is the view screen?" said Daisy.

Nau looked up from under a pile of circuit boards and wires he was happily rummaging through beneath a console. "They have holo-screens. No fixed position, just wherever's good. Lovely job."

"I want holo-screens. Why don't we have holo-screens? How do we turn it on?"

"Just ask the computer."

"What?"

"The ship's computer has a voice activated interface," explained Tongue. "Computer, activate holo-screen. Replay ship's log from entry to the Jagrapax star system."

"View screen activated," said a disembodied, calm, professional voice.

Daisy raised her eyebrows. "I want a voice activated computer interface. Why don't we have a voice activated computer interface?"

"Ah," said Nau, "Well, we do but . . . well, it's a pain in the spuds, if you know what I mean."

"Um, nope?"

A blue oblong fizzed into existence in the air before them, revealing the handsome, lined face of a middle-aged man with greying hair.

"Captain's log supplemental, Commodore Commode reporting," said the floating face. "We have arrived for our rendezvous with Space Scrap 17. They have signalled that they are running late but will be with us shortly. Only to be expected of a third-rate crew aboard a fifth-rate ship I suppose."

"Bit rude," said Daisy.

"I hear the XO is a complete moron."

"Oh, bitch. What does he say about the rest of the crew?"

"But the captain makes this guy look like a genius. She's so incompetent —"

"Computer, skip forward one minute," said Daisy. "Tittle tattle," she said in answer to Tongue's raised eyebrow, "Bit unprofessional if you ask me."

The log resumed playing. "She's a total klutz —"

"Computer skip forward another minute."

"— so stupid she can't —"

"Computer skip forward five minutes."

"— she'd probably exit a wormhole in the centre of a sun —"

"Oh, screw you Commodore!" Daisy's fist swiped ineffectively through the holo-image.

"But their late arrival does at least give us the chance to check an anomaly. Three of the four planets in this system seem to have been pulverized. Our Xeroxian science officer, Doctor Bizarre, is analysing the system for probable cause —" the commodore paused as an urgent voice broke in from across the bridge. He looked surprised. "You sure, Doctor? You're not hallucinating due to one of your weird alien mating cycles again, are you?" The other voice said something angry in reply. "Well, I don't know Doctor, last time you were on heat you said some very strange things about cheese . . . yes, right, fine. Helm set course to investigate." The commodore's attention returned to the screen, "It seems the fourth planet is now also breaking up and is enveloped in some kind of hard radiation. We're going to investigate. Commodore out."

The screen went blank for a moment. Then the face re-appeared.

"Captain's log supplemental supplemental. By the time we arrived at the fourth planet, there was nothing left but rubble. We spotted something leaving the system and have set course to pursue. Doctor Bizarre has projected its trajectory. He says it is on course for the Ululation system. I would have asked for more details, but I had to have him removed from the bridge after he started humping the chairs."

Daisy's eyes widened as she recalled the sticky substance she had dipped her fingers in. Discretely, she rubbed her hand on her overalls.

"But clearly," the commodore was saying,

"someone is trying to make damn sure these talks don't go ahead. Commodore out."

"Well, that settles it," said Tongue, "Someone wants to sabotage these talks so badly they are prepared to send a planet buster to do it. Captain, we need to get to the Nonsense Sphere and warn them."

Before Daisy could respond, the holo-screen reactivated. The commodore's face looked tense. "Something just ripped us out of hyperspace. We're in the Cuk system. Another planet has been ripped to pieces." He looked up in alarm. "What the hell is that?!"

#

"What the buggering flaps is that?!" Jones shouted at the view screen, which showed a huge, long, black tube with a gaping, glowing maw at one end like a doorway to hell, if doorways were made of mouths. The tube tapered down to a narrow point at the other end. It looked like an ice cream cone, thought Jones. A big, nasty, planet eating ice cream cone. Or a massive —

"It's big," said Steve, "about five miles long."

"Just entered the system at far range," said Mic.

"And headed in our direction," said Steve.

"Jeebuzz it looks like a nightmare," said Jones.

"Do you think?" said Steve. "I thought it looks more like a . . ."

"Yes?"

"Well, a giant turd."

"What?"

"You know, a turd. A floater."

"Yes exactly, the stuff of nightmares."

"You have nightmares about five-mile-long turds?"

"Well, I bloody well will now!" Jones stood from the captain's chair and walked over to stand before the view screen. He turned to the comms station, his visage framed by the gaping maw of the alien death machine. "Mic, contact the captain. Tell her we have engaged . . . the turd."

ON THE BRIDGE of the Square Jaw, Daisy and Tongue had finished reviewing the logs.

"So, let me get this straight," said Daisy, "This Doomsday Machine rips the Square Jaw out of hyperspace, attacks them and when the commodore realises all his weapons are useless against it, he and his crew abandon ship for the safety of the nearest planet."

"Yes," said Tongue.

"And he does this after witnessing the Doomsday Machine ripping planets apart."

"Yes."

"And then the commodore is surprised when the Doomsday Machine proceeds to rip the planet apart."

"Yes."

"Twat."

"Yes. Although, to be fair, Xeroxian's are mildly telepathic. If Doctor Bizarre was in a mating cycle, his psychic trauma could have infected the rest of the crew. We need to return to Space Scrap 17. If Doctor Bizarre was right about that thing's course, it is imperative we get to the Nonsense Sphere and warn the Ululations."

"Captain," said the computer, "We are receiving an incoming transmission from Space Scrap 17."

"Let's hear it, Computer," Daisy said, smiling. "I like this, I'm going to activate our computer's voice interface when we get back."

"Captain, this is Mic Vol. XO reports that we have engaged a turd."

"What the hell is he talking about Mic?"

"I believe he is referring to the planet killer."

"What?"

"Which has just re-entered the system."

"What?"

"And is on course to intercept us."

"What?"

"Oh. And is now shooting at us."

"WHA -" the lights suddenly dimmed as the bridge shook alarmingly and alarms alarmed alarmingly. A panel exploded in a shower of sparks and the three crewmen in their artificial bodies were thrown to the floor.

"Jeebuzz!" shouted Daisy.

Chief Nau was furiously punching at some buttons on a console.

"Computer, give us an external view," shouted Tongue.

A holo-screen fizzed into existence. It showed the approach of a huge, gaping maw. They watched in stunned silence, braced for a fiery death. But at the last moment the thing veered off, firing its vast energy beam impotently into the blackness of space.

"What is it firing at?" asked Tongue.

"Nothing," said Nau, "Or rather, it thinks it's firing at another Square Jaw. I'm using the holo-projectors to generate an external image. It's chasing a ghost. Should give us time to get back."

"Excellent work Mr Nau," said Tongue.

"Computer open a channel to Space Scrap 17," said Daisy.

"Channel open."

"Mic, Chief Nau has distracted the planet buster. Get us the hell back."

After a moment Smiert's voice came over the intercom. "Captain, ready to transfer. Who first?"

"Tongue, then Nau, then me."

"Transfer activated."

The body that Tongue had occupied stiffened and then collapsed backward, an empty shell once more.

The bridge shook again. Terminals exploded around them in a shower of sparks.

"Well as distractions go, that didn't last long," said Daisy, picking herself up from the floor. The holo-screen showed the alien death machine bearing down on Space Scrap 17.

"Chief, can we get this ship moving?"

"We can manoeuvre. The Ion engines might make Mark 1. Maybe. The wormhole generators were completely flat but I've got them on charge. Be ready in about fifteen minutes."

"Fifteen minutes? I'm not sure we've got fifteen seconds! If only we had some weapons."

"Oh, I've got weapons systems online. Not much left of them though. There's a couple of anti-matter swarms and a pulse cannon is still working."

"Good enough, well done. Fire an anti-matter swarm and shoot that bastard with the pulse cannon."

"Won't even scratch that thing. Its hull is pure neutronium. Lovely job."

"Neutronium?"

"Well, when the core of a white dwarf star exceeds its Chandrasekhar limit —"

Daisy cut him off. "Long story short please Chief."

"It's dense. We can't hurt it."

"Maybe not. But we can distract it from our ship, yes?"

"Right you are guv, swarm launched. Manoeuvring into cannon range."

The holo-screen showed hundreds of tiny pinpricks as the swarm raced toward its target.

"In range."

"OK, let's flush this turd. Fire pulse cannon."

Pulses of light shot away from the Square Jaw, impacting on the hull of the Doomsday Machine at the same time as hundreds of anti-matter missiles exploded.

"Any effect?"

"Bugger all. Although it's stopped chasing the ship."

"Great."

"And now it's coming for us."

"Bollocks. Mic, get us back."

"Aye Captain, transferring Chief Nau."

The chief straightened and his rigid, artificial body crashed backward to the deck.

"Computer, evasive manoeuvres — keep us away from that thing."

#

In the captain's chair on the bridge of Space Scrap 17 Jones chewed on a knuckle. He took a deep breath and keyed the intercom. "Smiert, what's the hold up? Where's the captain?"

"Still on Square Jaw. We've lost computer connection."

"Mic?"

"Sorry sir, that last shot set off a cascade failure. Data packets can't be formed."

"Effect repairs."

"Yes XO, the thought had occurred to me."

"Do we still have audio?"

"Yes, radio is still effective."

"Patch me through."

"Channel open."

"Daisy, what's going on over there?"

"Well, I'm still here for one thing. The turd is coming after the Square Jaw. Any slight, remote possibility of you getting me back before that thing turns this ship into vapour?"

"We're working on it. Data transfer is

inoperative."

"Oh good . . . great. Michigan, I don't know what to do!"

Jones recognised that tone in her voice. Now that she was alone, she was starting to second guess herself, allowing events to crush her self-confidence. Such as it was.

"Yes, yes you do, you do know what to do Captain, you're doing great."

"I'm really not!"

"Listen, when you requested transfer back you said 'Tongue, Nau and then me', remember?"

"So?"

"That was the right call — mission specialist with the key information, engineer to make sure we can get out of here and put that information to use and then you. And then when that thing was coming for us, you distracted it, yes?"

"Yes but —"

"You made command decisions in the heat of battle. You didn't panic, you didn't second guess yourself, you made the decisions. Listen," he lowered his voice so the rest of the bridge crew could not hear. "You don't need an exam pass or a rule book. You made those decisions. You."

"Well, if you put it that way," she said after a brief

pause, "I do sound a bit captainy don't I? No, who am I kidding. That was a fluke. We're all dead and it's all my fault."

A sudden thought occurred to Jones. "Well, I wasn't going to mention it, but it might interest you to know that the doctor says she saw odd patterns when she transferred you over. Almost like, and I quote, 'two merged brain patterns'. Daisy — Captain — I don't think the neural uploader entirely cleared out Captain Weaver."

"What? Oh, that bloody black market cheap piece of shit!"

"Yes, but think about it. Heat of battle. Command decisions. Merged brain patterns."

"So, you think I did that because I'm thinking like her, like Captain Weaver?"

"Exactly."

"The notorious, murdering, psychotic, pirate Captain Weaver?"

"Yes."

"So, I'm a racist now?"

"Well, a Xenophobe. But you're alive. And so are we."

"No, that makes more sense. I'm doing captainy stuff because I have a real captain living in my head. Right, so we should —"

Daisy's voice cut out in a blizzard of static.

"Steve, what's happening?"

"The turd thing. It's firing on the Square Jaw."

\#

Daisy stood alone in her artificial body on the bridge of the battered LASS Square Jaw.

"Computer, how are the shields holding up?"

"Shields at thirty-seven per cent capacity. Tactically we cannot survive a direct impact from the alien weapon. However, indirect impacts are survivable. I have selected vectors in my evasive manoeuvres calculated to ensure we do not present a direct target."

OK. Bumpy ride but survivable.

"Computer, how long since my brain waves were downloaded into this body?"

"One hour and ten minutes."

Daisy updated her assessment. OK. Bumpy ride but survivable. For fifty minutes. After which her real body would die.

The bridge rocked again. "Shields at thirty-five per cent capacity. Reinforcement to forty per cent in seven minutes."

"Great, keep it up."

"Engines are beginning to overheat due to continued vector adjustment."

"Computer, do you understand the concept of a good news sandwich? I like good news sandwiches. They're the best. Although, fried egg sandwiches are pretty awesome."

"Please restate query."

"Never mind."

If the engines failed, the Square Jaw would be a sitting duck.

"OK, let's try to find some good news. Computer. Analysis of current and previous engagements with the alien weapon. Focus on proximity and pursuit tactics. Give me schematics on holo-screen."

The bridge rocked once more.

"Shields at thirty-four per cent. Reinforcement to thirty-seven per cent in twelve minutes."

Daisy needed to buy time.

And time was a resource in very limited supply.

#

"And this is it, is it?" Jones looked up from the DEVICE. Steve shrugged.

"Well, we got rid of everything else when the contract for the sewage transport came through.

"Right, fine, load them up." He was disappointed with Space Scrap 17's array of weapons, or rather 'potential' weapons, since she wasn't supposed to actually fight anything. He punched the engineering intercom.

"Chief, how's it going down there?"

"Just about done. We've removed the safeties, made the navigation MASER arrays as hot as we can. But we'll be lucky if they can boil an egg, let alone damage that thing."

"We don't need to damage it, just distract it from the Square Jaw. How about making it chase ghosts again?"

"We don't have holo-projectors."

"No, of course not. We don't have much of anything, do we? Well hurry up with the MASERs. Bridge out. Mic, communication arrays?"

Mic stopped what he was doing.

"Difficult to say. I've been waving this tool that makes beeping noises at the relays for a while now. I'm not sure it's making a difference or even if the relays actually like having tools beep at them."

"It's a digital synaptic re-router," said Tongue from the Mission Operations station, "When it stops beeping it will have finished rerouting the computer's neural pathways around the damaged communication motherboard. Keep waving until it stops."

"Increase waving," said Jones to Mic, "We've only got forty minutes until the captain's brain turns into jelly. Tongue," he made his way over to the Mission Ops station. "Anything else you can tell me about that Doomsday Machine? Other than it's invulnerable and can kill planets without breaking a sweat?"

Tongue waved his hands in the air, "It's invulnerable and kills planets without breaking a sweat. That's the only thing I can glean from the Square Jaw logs."

"Both an immovable object and an irresistible force," said Mic.

"Quite," said Tongue. "In any case, Doomsday Machine is a good description. An automated, robot weapon that must never be used because if you do, it's doomsday for everyone. Rather like the atomic weapons of your twentieth century."

"A flap sight worse than that," said Jones. "That thing makes nukes look like a sensible first option in response to a stroppy comment. No, this is more like the social media platforms of the twenty-first century."

Tongue shuddered. The Earth had been monitored for years by the Reptillions, whose brief was to watch for signs that the human race was about to develop the technology that would allow it to leave its solar system. In that event, the Reptillions were to warn the rest of the galaxy so that everyone could evacuate to Andromeda. It was only after the human race disarmed all its social media platforms, thereby proving that it did actually have some intelligence after all, that the threat from Earth was downgraded from 'Lethal, poisonous scum' to 'Morons'. At that point Fisticon J'al Raz Patralax, leader and chief coordinator of the Reptillion task force, shed his human outer skin disguise, which he had fondly named after his mother, D'vidi'ck, and left the Earth. Tongue shuddered again.

"Bridge?" Chief Nau's voice called out from the intercom.

"Go ahead."

"All done. MASERs are as hot as I can make them."

"Great. Standby. Steve how's it going with the torpedo tubes?"

"If by torpedo tubes you mean forward airlocks, all loaded."

"Right." Jones strode over to the captain's chair and sat down. "Get ready. We're going to throw everything we've got at that bastard. We've got to stop it shooting at the Square Jaw. Steve, get us as close as possible."

Daisy's analysis of the Square Jaw tactical logs had proved worthwhile. With the help of the computer, she observed that the alien weapon had proximity sensitivity. Anything within a certain area, say one hundred miles, it attacked. Which meant all she had to do was keep the Square Jaw over a hundred miles away from it and it wouldn't try to shoot them. Which was a problem because she couldn't get the distance due to the fact the death turd was capable of more speed than the damaged engines of the Square Jaw could muster.

"Captain Daryl, the alien weapon is veering off."

"What? Why?"

"It is now focused on Space Scrap 17."

"Damnit. Show me."

A holo-screen sprang up before her. She gasped.

The screen showed streaks of light flashing out from her ship, stabbing at the alien death machine.

"What are they shooting with? We don't have lasers or energy weapons."

"I have enhanced the display to provide visual representation of MASER fire. Space Scrap 17 is using navigation MASERs to attack the alien. MASER intensity is far beyond the recommended safety rating for such a vessel."

"They're hitting it with everything they've got but the kitchen sink."

"Correction. Space Scrap 17 is now discharging a large quantity of kitchen sinks at the alien."

"Sorry, what?"

"Space Scrap 17 is currently firing upon the alien with navigation MASERs and a large quantity of kitchen sinks discharged from their forward air locks."

Daisy regarded the screen again. Between the streaks of light, she could discern packing crates, helpfully enhanced by the computer with silver outlines.

"I don't suppose the alien is allergic to kitchen sinks?"

"Not noticeably. MASER fire is also proving ineffectual. However, the alien has stopped pursuing us. We are now able to create the distance we need to keep us out of its proximity detectors. Space Scrap 17 is now caught in a tractor beam and is being dragged into the maw of the alien weapon."

"No, see, that's a bad news sandwich. That's bad news, good news, bad news. I want — oh never mind."

"In two minutes, we will be outside the alien's proximity radius."

Daisy chewed her lip. Then she strode to the captain's chair and sat, her posture ramrod straight. "Computer, bring us within one hundred miles of the alien. Full engine burn. Arm anti-matter swarm and pulse cannon."

"Captain Daryl, proximity will make us a target within point blank range. Our weapons have proven ineffective against the alien."

"Quite right computer. And from here on in you can call me Captain Weaver."

If the computer had been programmed to notice such things it might have been disturbed by the manic gleam that had suddenly appeared in Daisy's eyes.

#

"XO, the tractor beam has cut off. We're free," said Steve.

"Great. Why? Are we dead? Did it shoot us with a massive energy beam so hard our consciousness hasn't caught up the fact we're now just atoms floating around thinking we're still alive?"

"It's the Square Jaw — it's having a stare off with the Doomsday Turd."

"What? Is she insane? Mic, get me Daisy — the captain."

"Waving and beeping," said Mic from below the comms station.

"Steve, get me the captain."

Steve punched the buttons on his board in his customary fashion — which is to say he blindly flapped his hands over the controls like someone hoping to hit the right buttons. Which he invariably did. "OK, comms open."

"Daisy! What are you doing?"

"Your captain is saving her ship, XO. Or rather Captain Weaver is saving my ship."

"Captain Weaver?! Oh Jeebuzz, look, Daisy —"

"No time — veer off and proceed to the Nonsense Sphere. You have to warn the Ululations."

"But Captain —"

"You have your orders. Captain out."

Jones stared at the view screen. What had he done? He felt a hand on his shoulder and heard Tongue's voice.

"She's right Jones. We have to warn them. She's bought us time."

"She's going to get herself killed and it's all my fault."

Tongue frowned. "Why would you say that? Wait, what did she mean about Captain Weaver?"

Jones's shoulders slumped. "She was alone on that ship. Beginning to panic. Look, Tongue," Jones lowered his voice, "She didn't pass the captain's exam."

"Yes, she did, you can't fake those certificates."

"Well, she did but it wasn't her. It . . . she bought a mind patch from the black market."

"But that technology is dangerous, it is outlawed in all —"

Jones waved away Tongue's objections, "Well she did. The patch personality was . . . was Captain Weaver."

"Wow. But I still don't see what —"

"To keep her from panicking, to give her hope, I told her the doctor reported two brain patterns when she completed the transfer. Like Daisy had two brain patterns instead of one."

"But that's nonsense, only an idiot would believe . . . oh."

"Yes, 'oh'. Daisy believes she has Captain Weaver's mind and experience. She thinks she's Captain Weaver."

"Oh Jones, what have you done?"

"Exactly."

"Well . . . irrespective of how we got here, she has bought us time. We need to warn the Ululations. We need to leave. Now."

Jones continued staring at the main viewer for a moment. "Damn it," he muttered. "Mic, has that wand thing stopped beeping? Can we transfer the captain back?"

"Afraid not sir."

"Damn it," he muttered again. The bridge crew seemed to hold their collective breath as they waited for his decision. Hating himself he said, "Steve, move us to a safe distance and bring the wormhole genera-tors online."

Jones enjoyed the XO position because it meant he could tell people what to do and he could sit back doing nothing. For once he hated the job. Slumped in the captain's chair — her chair — he had nothing to occupy his mind while the others went about their work.

"Steve, keep the Square Jaw on the main viewer."

The view screen shifted from the star studded blackness of space to the not so titanic battle between a tiny, damaged spaceship and a gigantic, planet-eating bastard.

"Jones, she's firing on the turd!" shouted Steve.

"She's what? Zoom in."

There was a flurry of pulse cannon fire, followed by a blinding explosion as her remaining anti-matter swarm futilely detonated. The alien responded with a vast, mile-wide energy weapon discharge.

When the static cleared there was no trace of the LASS Square Jaw.

Jones's fingernails bit into his palms. With a conscious effort he un-balled his fists. "Wormhole generator status?" he eventually said into the quiet that had descended on the bridge. "Steve!"

Steve jerked and tore his attention from the view screen. He glanced down at his board. "Wormhole generators ready. Exit point set for Ululation homeworld."

"Good. Bring us as close as you dare to that turd and fire MASERs. Then open the wormhole and get us out of here. Make sure the wormhole entrance is big enough for that thing to fit into."

"Sorry, what?"

"Just do it."

Tongue was suddenly standing before him. "The captain just saved us so we can get to the Ululations and warn them. You're throwing that away!"

"No, I just want to get that thing's attention."

"It will follow us!"

"It is headed that way anyway! We're faster, we'll get there ahead of it."

"But — why?"

"That thing just killed Daisy. I'm going to repay the favour. Now get back to your post, Mr Tongue."

For a moment, Tongue looked like he was going to protest further. But then he seemed to think better of it and went back to his station.

"For what it's worth," said Mic, "The beeping thing has stopped beeping."

Jones glared at Mic. Great. Now they could bring Daisy back. Except now there was no Daisy to bring back. His glare remained fixed on Mic as he said, "Steve, how are the MASERs?"

"Ready."

"Fire," said Jones.

Space Scrap 17 hurtled toward the alien

weapon, intense bursts of photons in the form of microwaves stabbing ineffectively at the giant artefact. The ship then veered off and streaked away in the opposite direction. Space Scrap 17 disappeared inside the now vast wormhole entrance.

After a moment, the Doomsday Machine followed.

IN A SMALL ROOM on a large island on the planet known as the Nonsense Sphere, an Ululation sat composing a sexy communication to his partner, who was at that moment in her bedroom, far away on one of the four major continents of that world. His message began 'My dearest SwishySkirt', before continuing with various flowery declarations of his love, the tone of which started at the ethereal end of the spectrum before proceeding rapidly to the more graphically biological end. His communication signed off with a rather unsatisfying 'all my love, QuiveringFetlocks'. He paused for a moment, considering, his digital pen raised. Then he nodded to himself, having discerned the necessary poetic flourish with which to round off his saucy missive. He bent once more to his digital paper and added,

'P.S. For your consideration, please find attached a photograph of my penis. Best wishes to your mother'. Yes, he thought, perfect. He clicked the top of his pen three times and the content of his digital paper translated itself into a quantum packet and sped off to SwishySkirt.

QuiveringFetlocks had a largely boring job that required him to be isolated on the island for long periods. Which wasn't so bad since, as an Ululation, he was quite keen on isolation. But his job isolated him even further by requiring him to stay inside, in this room packed with quietly humming computer equipment which he was required to sit and watch for long shifts and which was, to say the least, stultifyingly dull.

He was a member of the Ululation Space Corps, a military organisation whose main task was to ensure that the Ululation world remained isolated from the rest of the galaxy. The motto of this ancient and venerable institution, 'Fuck off', left no room for misinterpretation on this point and, to the minds of the creative team paid to come up with it, got the message across quite nicely.

QuiveringFetlocks's part in passing on this message to the rest of the galaxy was, like that of several other low-grade Ululations posted on various islands around the Sphere in rooms just like this one, to monitor the deep space tracking equipment for signs of incursion into Ululation space by aliens. Or to give them their proper military nomenclature, 'bastards'.

Writing erotic communications to his partner was one way in which QuiveringFetlocks staved off the boredom. The other was biscuits. He was quite fond of biscuits. But then who wasn't?

QuiveringFetlocks sat up abruptly, his hand frozen midway to a plate of lunch biscuits.

His signal monitoring boards had suddenly lit up like a Gavin Starmane parade.

He ran a diagnostic loop. No. The signal was real. This was it, the big one! He licked his prehensile upper lip nervously. Was this really it? If he raised the alarm and it was just a failed circuit . . . He ran the diagnostic once more. The equipment was working perfectly. Well then.

He stabbed at the big, red button.

"Yes?" said a terse voice.

By Starmane it was her! It had to be. Black-Window herself.

"Ma'am, this is monitor station Snicker three."

"Yes?" came the voice again, this time somehow

managing to convey hints of both impatience and impending, horrifyingly cruel violence.

He licked his lips once more. "Code Bastard."

There was a brief pause on the other end. "You're sure?"

"It's a true signal. As far as I can tell there is an unauthorised incursion at the edge of our system."

"Continue monitor and recording." The line went dead.

QuiveringFetlocks took a deep, shuddering breath. Ignoring the plate on his desk he opened the special draw, the draw that he had never in his wildest dreams expected to open.

QuiveringFetlocks reached tremulously into the draw for the excitement biscuits.

#

At the edge of the Testiculon binary star system, the home system of the isolationist Ululations, a fanfare of pyrotechnics announced the opening of a wormhole.

Space Scrap 17 bolted from the wormhole exit as if fleeing all the demons of hell. Which it sort of was.

"We're out of the wormhole," reported Steve.

"Excellent. All stop. Close the wormhole."

"But that thing is still in there!"

"I know. Now close the flapping wormhole."

Steve grinned and shut down the wormhole generators. Immediately, the wormhole exit collapsed.

Tongue stepped down to stand by Jones. "You've trapped it in hyperspace."

"Yes."

"With no way out."

"No."

"Oh, now that's clever."

"I was aiming," said Jones, sitting back with a sadistic grin, "for vindictive and hateful, but I'll take clever."

"Mic, raise Ululation military command on the Nonsense Sphere at once," said Tongue, his tone urgent.

"What's up?" said Jones.

"They will have detected our arrival, which means they'll be preparing to blow us to atoms."

"But we've just saved them from a giant, alien doomsday weapon."

"They don't know that. Yet."

"But they must be expecting someone — the Square Jaw was . . ." Jones trailed off, his feeling of elation at the destruction of the alien weapon replaced by the harsh memory of Daisy's death.

Tongue placed an awkward hand on Jones's arm, "The Square Jaw had a set of agreed authorisation codes to be transmitted continuously as they approached this system. Without those we are just trespassers in their space."

"Unable to contact the Ululations," said Mic. "That odd radiation is scattering our signal."

"How?" said Tongue. "That should have died with the alien weapon."

"Correlation does not imply causation?" said Mic, somehow managing a shrug in his environment suit.

"What does that imply?" said Steve, pointing at the view screen.

Outside, space-time bent like light caught in a particularly twisted and massive gravity lens. And then, like so much wet tissue paper, it ripped open. The alien doomsday weapon thundered back into normal space through the tortured space-time fracture, hungry and looking for something, preferably several somethings, to kill.

Jones stood, eyes wide, "Holy mother of —"

"Impossible!" Tongue's hair wrapped itself around his neck, as if seeking comfort.

"Well, that's it then," said Steve, "we're dead."

"XO, I'm receiving a transmission!" said Mic.

"From the Doomsday Machine? Is it asking for terms of surrender? We surrender, tell it we surrender."

"It'll be the Ululations," said Tongue stepping forward, "tell them to direct their attack at —"

"It's Captain Daryl."

"No it isn't," snapped Jones, "Not unless she's speaking from beyond the grave."

"She's speaking from the bridge of the Square Jaw actually."

"What? Mic, start making sense, the Square Jaw's atoms are scattered across what remains of the atoms of the Cuk system."

"Space Scrap 17, do you read? I'm boosting my signal to punch through the interference, the tech on this ship is amazing," Daisy's voice crackled from the intercom.

"Daisy — Captain — where are you?"

"Had to find somewhere this bastard couldn't shoot at me. I hitched a ride."

"Jones, look," Steve pointed at the view screen where he had zoomed in on the tail end of the alien weapon. Squatting on the back of the Doomsday Machine was the LASS Square Jaw — in the only place in the galaxy safe from the alien energy weapons.

"I blinded it with the anti-matter swarm explosions and opened a wormhole above its back. I was already gone by the time it started shooting."

"Nice work! Listen, we finished repairs here, we can bring you back to your own body."

"Not yet XO, I need to kill this thing first."

"Captain," said Mic, "the alien weapon has by all measures been fashioned to be both an immovable object and an irresistible force. How do you intend to defeat it with nothing more than a wrecked spaceship?"

Daisy did not answer, instead a disconcerting dry cackle came over the intercom. "Do me a favour," she said, "Fire at this thing and then run as fast as you can for the Nonsense Sphere."

"Captain, the Ululation space force won't be able to take it on. They won't even slow it down. I recommend we try to lead it away from this system," said Tongue.

"In any case," said Jones, "You only have five minutes left before your brain turns to jelly over here."

"Well, you'd better be ready then. Now follow my orders. Captain out."

#

Moments later Space Scrap 17 opened fire on the alien weapon and shot off into space.

The alien war machine roared off in pursuit. Not that it needed much encouragement — it was headed that way anyway and it was already pissed off at being sealed in hyperspace.

That was the way Daisy imagined it anyway. She couldn't help but anthropomorphize her inadvertent host. It helped make it slightly less threatening, but only in so far as an angry tiger with a gun might seem slightly less threatening if you took away its gun.

It wasn't much, but it kept her from screaming.

"Daisy," Jones's worried voice sounded over the intercom, "Doctor Smiert says she's ready to transfer, but you only have two minutes and thirty-five seconds left."

"Stand by XO, we're going to be cutting it very fine. Computer?"

"Yes, Captain Weaver?"

"You have the coordinates worked out?"

"I do. However, I would remind the Captain of the danger —"

"Never mind. Activate wormhole generators."

One hundred miles ahead of the Doomsday

Machine, a wormhole entrance blossomed into existence with a crackle of exotic radiations and hyperphysics. The weapon's velocity meant it could not avoid thundering into the mouth of the wormhole.

Daisy imagined it didn't really care.

In fact, she was counting on it.

#

On the bridge of Space Scrap 17, all attention was fixed on the main viewer, which showed the vast alien weapon roaring after them in pursuit.

"What's that?" shouted Jones.

"Wormhole," said Steve, "She's opening a wormhole directly in its path!"

"Nice try," said Tongue, "but it won't buy us much time, that thing can tear itself back into real space."

"Er, Science Officer, can you check these wormhole coordinates?" Tongue exchanged a puzzled glance with Jones as he joined Steve and checked his board.

He blinked once. Twice.

"Bloody hell," he said simply.

"What? Bloody hell what?" Jones's nerves were

stretched to breaking point, the last thing he wanted was another variable to juggle.

"XO," came the doctor's urgent voice, "We have one minute twenty seconds."

"Daisy, we have to pull you back now."

"Not yet, XO," Daisy's voice crackled against the background radiation. "Just a few more seconds."

#

In the coldness of space, the alien war machine thundered toward the mouth of the wormhole.

Its programming did not care about this at all.

Its programming knew that once it exited the wormhole it could simply create its own and come right back here. Of course, they would not have been able to create an exit point in the middle of a hostile environment like, say, a star. Wormhole mouths could not be formed in such places, the exotic particles used to open normal space to hyperspace just could not stabilise in such intense environments. And in the event the wormhole exit was closed before it could leave hyperspace, well, it would just rip its way back into normal space.

Like anything else in this galaxy, this was nothing it couldn't handle.

Out of mild curiosity, it checked the wormhole exit point.

Oh, it thought.

Bugger.

#

The bridge crew on Space Scrap 17 watched in fascinated horror as the view screen relayed events.

They watched as the mighty Doomsday Machine thundered into the wormhole, thrust headlong by its own unstoppable velocity.

They watched as, at exactly the same time it entered the wormhole, the Doomsday Machine also exited it.

And crashed into itself coming in.

Daisy had programmed the wormhole exit to occupy almost exactly the same space as the entrance.

No sooner did the weapon enter the wormhole, it also came out again.

Right into its own unstoppable path.

"XO, bring me back," shouted Daisy over the intercom.

"Now Doctor, bring her back!"

They watched the view screen as the Doomsday

Machine violently shattered into itself, its atoms exploding away from each other at almost the speed of light.

"Immovable object, allow us to introduce irresistible force," muttered Mic.

The view screen whited out, sensors unable to cope with the tumultuous explosive devastation on display.

BY THE TIME Jones got down to sick bay Daisy was already sitting up, a bottle of water gripped in both hands. She gave him a wan smile.

"Welcome back, Captain," he said. He could not keep the grin from his face. He didn't grin very often but when he did, he found his face was the best place to keep it. Although he felt he could keep a passable grin on his elbows if he concentrated really hard, which he didn't like to do as it gave him a headache.

Daisy frowned down at the water bottle. "This water tastes of blue," she said.

Jones looked over at the doctor who was tidying away the neural uploader. "Is she . . . you know," he made vague gestures around his head.

"I'm perfectly fine thank you XO, just feels weird being back in my own body."

"This is normal after such a procedure," said Smiert, laying a reassuring hand on Daisy's arm.

"Thank you, Doctor, that's very reassuring."

Smiert shrugged, "It is? Oh. Good. Well, we go with that then. Now, please leave sick bay."

"Wait, shouldn't you run tests?"

"Tests? No Captain, I am positive I want you to leave sick bay." Smiert went back to packing away the equipment.

Daisy frowned. "Where was it you said you qualified, Doctor?"

Smiert paused, holding up a pair of electrodes. "Where did you say you got this neural uploader, Captain?"

"Yes well," said Daisy quickly, sliding off the gurney, "That will be all Doctor, thank you. Jones, what's happening?"

"Well, you did it. The rest of the bridge crew are still pointing and laughing at what remains of the Doomsday Turd. Which isn't much. That was brilliant, opening a wormhole exit inside an entrance. Fantastic. You did . . . you did do that on purpose, didn't you? That wasn't, like, your attempt at navigation that went horribly, horribly wrong was it?"

"No XO, that was the plan."

"Good. Of course. Yes. But just in case, you are

banned from going anywhere near the helm in future."

"It was the computer that did all the maths, not me. Which reminds me, I want our computer switched to voice activation. So much more efficient."

"I'll tell Mic to sort it. Brilliant idea that."

"Oh well, you know what they say. Two heads are better than one."

"What do you mean?" asked Smiert.

Jones coughed. "Yes, well, I think we've over-stayed our lack of welcome in sick bay, shall we —" Jones indicated the exit.

"Well, you know Doctor. You discovered I have two sets of brain waves."

"That is not possible. You have one set of brain-waves like everyone else."

"No. Two. Jones, didn't you say . . ." She looked questioningly at Jones.

"Right, yes, about that. See, you were stuck over there and there was this huge killing machine thing, and it was all a bit bonkers and stuff. Still, all worked out, shall we go?"

"You lied?"

"A white lie, a small lie, in fact not a lie at all, because you are so like Captain Weaver, you could be the same person and . . . Captain? Daisy?"

Daisy stood motionless, a rictus grin frozen on her face, eyes glazed, staring into the abyss of reality which now pointed back and laughed at her.

"Daisy?"

She took a deep breath and released a star shattering scream of pent-up terror.

#

Tongue entered his cabin and locked the door. He extracted his briefcase and opened it. The isomorphic sensors recognised that this was indeed Ambassador NotPronounceableByYourPrimitive-EarthTongue and that it should not kill him. Which it was somewhat disappointed at since it really didn't get much action these days.

With brisk professionalism and practised movements, Tongue opened the case and activated the internal secret locks. The atoms of the bottom of the case rearranged themselves, revealing the essential tools of his craft. Hairbrush, a gun, industrial strength pheromone aftershave, a gun, lippy, a gun and a credit coin containing unlimited funds in any currency. And a gun. There were one or two other items vital to a man in his profession, including an encrypted transceiver that he now selected. He paused briefly, wondering if on second thoughts it would have been wiser to bring some ammunition for the guns but there was really no room for it. Not if he were to have sufficient supplies of emergency makeup. Shrugging, he closed the case again and activated the transceiver.

Instantly a privacy bubble enveloped him, ensuring that his conversation could not be accidentally or intentionally overheard.

The voice, when it came, was as Tongue remembered. Like multiple sibilant voices speaking at once, but each slightly out of synch with the other. All the voices shared the same qualities: mocking, ancient and malevolent, like evil rocks grinding evilly against one another. "Speak, Agent Rebus."

Tongue's throat was suddenly dry. He swallowed hard. "Interception of the Square Jaw successful. However, weapon was destroyed."

"How?"

"Wormhole manipulation."

"Ah. And the Ululation homeworlds?"

"Remain intact."

"It appears we underestimated the command crew of Space Scrap 17."

"I don't think that's possible. They're idiots."

"Then explain how it came to be that they destroyed an indestructible weapon?"

Fair enough. They had him there. "I can't. But I still don't understand what the point of all this was? You assigned me to assassinate the Ululation delegates. Why use the alien doomsday weapon? If you wanted to destroy the Ululation home world, what was the point of my assassinating the delegates?"

He could almost feel a recoil in the voices, like snakes rearing back, about to strike. Had he gone too far?

"We did not expect to destroy the Nonsense Sphere — their shielding technology is too formidable. Which is why we wished to . . . dissuade them from joining the Association. But if the weapon had succeeded in doing so, so much the better. No, this was a demonstration of power to upset the Ululation isolationist factions who would object to the talks on the basis that such negotiations would bring them to the attention of devastating alien weapons. We intended that the Square Jaw would encounter the weapon and fight it. The weapon was to leave the ship dead but intact for others to find — we wanted witnesses to our power. If the Square Jaw had somehow survived, you were in place to ensure that the delegates would not. Their deaths, along with the alien weapon, would be more than enough to dissuade the Ululations from joining the Association. In light of the destruction of the weapon, you will proceed with your assigned task. Assassinate the Ululation delegates."

"But how? Their transport has been destroyed."

There came a sound like a chorus of evil chuckles. "Stand by for further instructions, Agent Rebus."

Miasma cut the communication channel and the privacy bubble collapsed.

Daisy had not expected a standing ovation from the crew. They clapped as she and Jones passed them in the corridor. They clapped as she entered the bridge. She wasn't quite sure what to do with her body under these circumstances. She'd certainly fantasised about such scenarios but as to facing them in real life? What does one do? Smile and nod? Wave? No, not wave, she wasn't a queen. Or was she? No! Stop it Daisy, she chided herself. Fine, not a queen . . . but she was pretty damn good though.

Her release of pent up fear and outright terror in the sick bay had left her feeling much relieved.

One thing about inhabiting the body of a Bloke was that it did not have an adrenaline system. Which meant all her fears and terrors were purely in her head. She wasn't governed by evolutionary fight or flight responses. Which had enabled her, reasoned the doctor, to think dispassionately and objectively, even under immense pressure. That was the reason she was able to defeat the undefeatable. Not this rubbish about two brain waves and being some kind of reincarnation of Captain Weaver.

However, all that changed once she had returned to her real body.

With her experiences so recent, there was nothing to stop her body undergoing a delayed adrenaline dump, nothing to prevent the onset of those fight or flight responses.

Which was why, in sequential order, she screamed, punched Jones in the face and ran around sick bay until she could be wrestled to the floor by Jones and the doctor could administer a mild sedative. As he desperately tried to hold on to Daisy's flailing limbs, Jones suggested to the doctor that it might be a good idea to administer a mild sedative to Daisy as well. Shrugging and with a sleepy smile on her face, the doctor did as he suggested.

Between the calming effects of the sedative, the fact that she had succeeded where a veteran captain of the flag-ship of the fleet had failed, the response of the crew to her return, the joyous relief that she and her crew, not to mention countless Ululations, were still alive, Daisy was feeling pretty damn good about herself. Which was not a feeling she was used to. Not at all. So, she had no idea how to respond to the applause of her crew. In the end, she decided just to go with it and grin, even if that did make her look like a ravenous serial killer on the prowl.

As the applause died down, the crew resumed their stations.

"What's our status, Mr Power?" said Daisy as she relaxed into the captain's chair. For the first time taking that seat, she did not feel like a fraud. Well, not a *total* fraud anyway.

"Damage report the size of an epic fantasy trilogy, Chief Nau crying into his oil rag, sewage cargo intact. But the discharge orifices still need some work."

"We have received an invitation from the Ululations to approach their planet. They offer," Mic inclined his head segment over his board, "yes, they offer congratulation biscuits. And repair facilities."

"Oh. Well, OK, Steve set course for the Nonsense Sphere."

"Course laid in."

"Right. Off we pop."

Steve's hand came down on the big green button.

"XO," Daisy turned to Jones, "Am I right in thinking we are the first — Jones, what the hell are you doing?"

What Jones was doing was standing by his station, injecting himself with a hypodermic. He looked up at her.

"Oh, relax Daisy. Captain. Daisy captain. I asked the good doctor for a stim."

"You're taking stims? On the bridge?"

"Yes, I'm taking stims on the bridge. I've been awake more than forty-eight hours, during which time I've unblocked a sewage treatment processor, witnessed what I thought was the horrible death of the woman I lo . . . I mean, a woman I look up to. At, the horrible death of a woman I look at. I've been in a battle with a giant psycho killer space turd and, and," Jones waved a finger at her for emphasis, "I haven't had a drink. That's a human rights fringe right there. Infringement. A clear infringement rights of human. And now, just when it looks like we can all have massive and ill-advised amounts of alcohol and a bit of a nap, now we're making first bloody contact with an isolationist race which could lead to all-out war or the polite exchange of biscuits of various delicious flavours, whatever the flaps that means. So yes, I'm taking stims."

"Were you about to say, 'the woman I love'?"

"What? No. Ridiculous. That would be insubordination."

"Uh-huh. Aren't you the least bit concerned about the side effects?"

"No, I'm sure there will be some. It'll be great."

"No XO, side effects are a bad thing."

"Nonsense! Are they? Wait," Jones called up the medication notes on his DEVICE. "Here they are. 'Big Pharma Amphetamine Fun Pack neural stimulants. Big Pharma accept no liability. Please contact customer service in the event you survive this medication as that's always nice to hear. To stave off the effects of tiredness or fatigue take one dose. Warning this stimulant may cause drowsiness.' What? No, wait, it doesn't say that. I was hallucinating. Ah, 'this stimulant may cause hallucinations'. OK, fair enough. 'Hallucinations, violent urination and excessive mood swings'. No, 'excessive urination and violent mood swings' . . . and there's some other words, Jeebuzz I hate words! Lazy bastards, why do I have to read them, why can't they read themselves I mean that's their job!" With a snarl, Jones threw the DEVICE across the room where it shattered against the wall. "Jeebuzz but I need a piss. Would anyone like a dance? Come on, we should all have a dance."

"Jones, why don't you go off-duty for a couple of hours," said Daisy. "Take a power nap. We can handle things here for a while."

"What? I can't sleep now, I've got too much energy! No, tell you what, I'll go and find the toilets, walk off some of this pep. And when I come back," Jones waggled a swaying finger at Daisy, "we'll discuss this further young man."

With that, Jones span on his heel and left the bridge.

"Captain," Tongue stepped down from the Mission Ops station to stand before Daisy. "We have received new mission parameters."

One day, Daisy thought, I'll understand comments like that. She put on her best serious face. "Have we. Oh. Good."

Tongue sighed and tried again. "There has been a change of plan."

"With you. OK, what's new pussycat?"

"What?"

Daisy gave a dismissive wave, "What's changed?"

"Although disturbed by the turn of events, the Ululation government was impressed by your destroying the alien weapon and consequent saving of Ululation lives. This has given the Association much honour in their eyes and convinced them to continue with the negotiations."

"OK, so the Association will send a new ship to pick up the delegates?"

"No Captain. The Ululations insist that their delegates be transported to Blah-Blah by Space Scrap 17. Anything less would be regarded as a breach of honour. Also, I suspect, they will feel safer aboard a starship that can prevail against alien doomsday weapons. And just in case we encounter any other hostile obstacles along the way, there is a squadron of Yerbootsian fighter ships en route to provide us escort."

"Oh. That's . . . nice. They do understand this is a bulk carrier for garbage, currently filled to the brim with liquid sewage, yes?"

"They do."

"How the hell are we supposed to accommodate them? We're not an Ambassador Class ship."

"They understand all of this. Space Scrap 17 is to transport the Ululations to Blah-Blah. The orders are confirmed by Association Command. Upon arrival at the Nonsense Sphere, the Ululations will assist with our most pressing repairs and transport the delegates aboard. I am to greet them and discuss pre-meeting schedules and agree agendas as I would have done aboard the Square Jaw."

Daisy sighed. "Oh well, doesn't sound like we have any say in this. Best overalls everyone — we're going to have company."

"CAPTAIN, we are currently in not crash around the planet Nonsense Sphere," announced Steve.

Daisy looked up from her DEVICE. "By 'not crash', do you mean 'orbit'?"

"Yes. Well as close as we can get to an orbit. We're usually just happy not to be crashing and leave it at that."

"I see. Mic, how's the computer voice activation coming?" Daisy was determined to have at least one impressive piece of technology on her ship and had been delighted to find that their computer had voice activation functionality.

"Are you sure that's a good idea?" Steve had asked when she suggested it.

"Yes, it's awesome. They had one on the Square Jaw. It's a huge time saver, you'll see."

"It's just we tried it once before and . . . well, the AI is a bit of an early version and we found it easier just to do stuff ourselves."

Daisy had waved his objections aside. It was cool and she wanted it and that was that.

Mic flicked a few switches. "Voice activation ready."

"Great. Do things 'n' stuff," she waved her arms vaguely in the air.

"Things and stuff?"

"Yes Mic, things 'n' stuff. Make voice activation happen. Thing the," she gestured again, "stuff."

"Ah," said Mic, "Activating voice activation. Voice activation active."

The bridge rocked as a shudder rippled through the ship.

"What was that?" Daisy asked, alarmed. "No wait, don't answer that. I'll do it. Computer," she said to the ceiling.

The voice, when it came, was grating and loud. Very, very loud. "WHAAAAT???"

"Ow! Mic!"

"Sorry, the sound card is, well, unsound to say the least."

"You're not kidding. Right, well Computer what was the cause of that buffeting just now?"

"LOOK," screamed the Computer, "I AM CURRENTLY PERFORMING TWO BILLION, THREE HUNDRED AND FIFTY-SIX MILLION, TWO HUNDRED AND THIRTY THOUSAND MIPS, A MIP, BY THE WAY, BEING DEFINED AS 'MILLION INSTRUCTIONS PER SECOND'! I REALLY DON'T HAVE TIME FOR THIS! NOW, I CAN DO LIFE SUPPORT OR TELL YOU THE CAUSE OF THE BUFFETING — WHICH IS IT?"

"Um, life support please."

"GOOD!"

Daisy pinched the bridge of her nose with her index finger and thumb. "Steve, does anything work properly on this ship?"

"Toilets."

"Oh. That's a relief."

"Well, the ones on W deck. If we use the ones on A deck, the engines go offline."

"GRAVITY FIELD!" screamed the Computer.

"Jeebuzz," hissed Daisy, her heart pounding.

"THERE'S A GRAVITY FIELD! IT'S A PLANET, WHERE THE HELL DID A PLANET COME FROM? OK, NOBODY PANIC, CALCULATING SPACIAL VECTORS! JEEBUZZ, DOES ANYONE KNOW HOW TO CALCU-

LATE SPACIAL VECTORS? NO, IT'S OK, I FOUND THE SUBROUTINE. I NOW HAVE SEVEN HUNDRED AND FIFTEEN MILLION MAJORLY STRESSFUL THINGS TO DO TO AVOID COLLISION! Computer out."

"OK, look, maybe this was a bad idea. Mic, turn off voice activation."

Mic and Steve exchanged glances.

"What?"

"Well," said Mic, "If I do that, it would require the computer to get involved and I don't think we want to give it another task just now."

"I can't have it bellowing a bloody status update every thirty seconds!"

"I can set the interaction level to zero?"

"Meaning?"

"It'll only speak when spoken to."

."Fine. That, do the thingy stuff that makes that happen."

"Captain, the Ululation shuttle is on approach," said Steve.

"OK. Tongue?"

"On my way," said Tongue moving briskly from the bridge.

An audio alert sounded on Steve's board. "Um . . ." he said.

"What? What's the beeping noise? Is that the 'everything is under control' alert?"

"Er," said Steve.

"Something else super good happening?"

"Well, are we defining 'good' as 'effluent orifices coming online and targeting the Ululation home world'? Because if we are, then this is exceptional."

"Oh, flapping flaps," Daisy jumped out of her chair. An effluent dump was the last thing she needed. Well, not the one that was happening now anyway.

"Tell them to stop, take them offline."

"Not responding."

"Computer, disable effluent orifices!"

"Unable to comply."

"Why?"

"BECAUSE I'M DOING SIXTEEN BILLION BINARY LOGIC COMPUTATIONS PER SECOND AND ALL OF THEM BADLY. OR BECAUSE THE CONTROL SYSTEMS WERE DAMAGED BECAUSE SOME IDIOT TRIED TO MANUALLY DOCK A CARGO POD AND IT SMASHED THE BASTARD THINGS INTO A MARMALADE OF NONSENSE. ONE OF THOSE."

Oh, Jeebuzz flaps.

"NOW WHAT'S THAT THING YOU PEOPLE DO WITH YOUR LUNGS?"

Daisy looked confused for a moment. "Er, breathe?"

"IS IT IMPORTANT?"

"Yes, very."

"RIGHT, I'D BETTER KEEP THE LIFE SUPPORT SYSTEMS GOING THEN?"

"Yes please."

"ANYTHING ELSE?"

"No, all good."

"FINE." With that, the computer fell silent.

"Steve try things and stuff. Shut down those orifices!"

"Tried. Failed."

"Reverse the polarity!"

"That doesn't mean anything."

"Steve, we are about to dump one hundred and sixty-eight million gallons of sewage onto the Ululation home world in the middle of delicate negotiations with a race who have a strict, not to say stressy, honour code. We have to do something!"

#

For the last half an hour, Jones had jogged

around the corridors of Space Scrap 17 burning with energy. He couldn't be sure of course but he suspected Doctor Smiert had deliberately supplied him with industrial grade stims. Cow.

He came to a stop, panting. He realised he was grinding his teeth. Again. With an effort he unclenched his jaw and un-balled his fists. He considered re-balling his fists and punching the wall. Then he considered doing so would likely break his knuckles thus preventing him from punching anything else, which would make him even more annoyed but unable to do anything about it.

No, he thought, best to find something softer to punch. That way he would never have to stop. A nasty grin etched itself on his face at that delightful thought.

Until now his jogging and perpetual movement had prevented him from noticing how desperately he wanted to pee. Now his brain could not help but notice the stack of unopened messages from his bladder marked 'most urgent', 'final demand' and 'are you taking the piss because seriously, someone has to!'.

Jones hopped from one foot to the other. Nearest toilet, nearest toilet, where — aha!

Below the sign reading 'DECK A' was another that said 'Toilets' with a helpful arrow.

Perfect. Jones jogged off in the indicated direction.

#

"Effluent release countdown has started," said Steve.

"Oh good," said Daisy, "That's lovely. Perfect."

"Might I suggest," said Mic, "that we move to a higher orbit? Perhaps leave orbit altogether?"

"Brilliant! Wait, are the delegates aboard?"

Steve checked his board. "Yes. Tongue is escorting them from the shuttle bay now."

"Fantastic. Steve, back us off, get us out of orbit."

"We haven't been cleared."

"Steve!"

"Right. Backing us off." Steve punched in the necessary vectors and hit the green button.

"Mic, get me the Ululation high command. I'll need to explain this. Somehow."

"Er, Captain we're not moving."

"Of course, we're moving Steve. Steve we are moving. Yes, we are. Why wouldn't we be moving?"

"Engines are offline."

"Flaps' sake!" Daisy hit the intercom. "Chief Nau, why are the engines offline?"

A creaky voice came over the intercom. "This is Mr Kettlewick. To whom am I speaking?"

"Kettlewick? This is the captain, put the chief on."

"Ah, I congratulate you on your high-pitched voice sir, not many men are capable of reaching such heights of falsetto delectation. As to the chief, I'm afraid he is no longer present. By which I mean he has used his time travel device in a doomed attempt to correct the problem of the effluent orifices in the past. Regrettably, as I pointed out to him, the temporal coordinator was damaged during our battle with the monster. He replied that fortune favours the bold. However true that may be, it appears fortune utterly despises the stupid, as Chief Nau is now then. Or is yet to be. But either way, regrettably not here. As to your inquiry regarding the engines, it appears that someone has used the flushing mechanism in the toilets on Deck A, thus kicking the engines offline. I have commenced the restart sequence. It will take five minutes to achieve functional readiness."

"Steve, how long until the orifices discharge?"

"Four minutes."

"Flaps! Kettlewick, you have three minutes to get the engines restarted."

"You think me a whore sir?! The process will take five minutes. No more and no less. This is science! Just as the laws of physics dictate it takes precisely five minutes to bring a woman to arousal, observing the specific and undeviating sequence of actions in the correct order and for the precise allocation of time, it will take five minutes for the engine restart process to complete. There is no circumvention of the procedure sir! Engineering out."

Daisy swallowed down on the panic rising within her. What was it the doctor had said? She was able to think objectively and clearly on the Square Jaw because there was no evolutionary psychology governing her biochemical reactions. Or rather there was, but the pseudo-carbon printed body of the Bloke she inhabited did not possess complex biochemical reactions. So, think clearly and objectively. She thought clearly. She weighed the situation objectively. She thought about her options both clearly and objectively and objectively and clearly. She came to a rational and objective and very clear conclusion.

"Nope. We're screwed."

"Ululation high command Captain," said Mic.

"What? No! Delay them, I need to think."

"On screen."

"Mic I said delay them not —"

"Greetings Captain Daryl. I am NickersGaily, High Mane of Ululation Central Herd."

Daisy regarded the view screen. It showed three elongated faces arranged in a triangular formation that seemed to float against a black background.

"Aha, yes, greetings o . . . Oh. You're a . . . you're . . . sorry, how would you describe your species?"

#

Jones left the bathroom on Deck A in the relaxed state of someone who had been staving off the urgent cries of a full bladder for way too long.

He desperately needed a shower and a change of clothes. He had grown fond of his T-shirt with its amusing cartoon zebra-punching logo and hoped to meet its owner at some point. Anyone who hated zebras like he did was clearly one of a select group and someone to get drunk with. Of course, such a meeting might mean he would have to return the T-shirt to its zebra-phobic owner, which he would regret, but in that event, he would wait until the mythical owner was blind drunk and then steal it. But all that would have to wait even though, given the exertions of the past few hours, the T-shirt was now more congealed sweat than tasteful attire.

No, he had a score to settle with that idiot doctor. Excessive urination? Violent mood swings? Grinding his teeth, he marched off in search of an elevator or lift or whatever they called them on this ship. He'd show her violent mood swings! And maybe some excessive urination for good measure.

#

"The designation you are looking for, Captain, is 'Zebroid'."

Daisy blinked at the view screen. "Huh. So that's, what, humanoid Zebra?"

The three faces inclined in various directions. "Bit human centric," said NickersGaily, "But yes, we evolved from an equine species. Or rather, two equine species. Originally the peoples of the Nonsense Sphere and our sister planet, the Scents Globe, were separate. Now our flesh is joined in the holy stripes, thanks to Gavin Starmane, our most revered hero."

"Revered," chorused the other Ululations.

"So, uh, what can I do for you, I'm afraid we are quite busy up here, what with things and stuff."

"Captain, we have received reports that your discharge orifices have targeted our planet. Specifically, our most sacred grasslands. We would like an explanation for this. StrangeGallop here," the Ululation occupying the bottom left of the triangle of Zebroid faces inclined its muzzle and raised a hoof, "wonders if this is an honorific custom of your people?"

"Ah," said Daisy, "yes, about that . . ."

#

Tongue was worried.

He had formally received the delegation at the shuttle bay and the three Ululations, introduced as PrancingHoof, FoamingWithers and AchingChestnuts, marvelled at the ship that had battled an alien super weapon in defence of a race that its crew had never met. Much honour, they said, was indeed owed to these representatives of the Loose Association.

Tongue had made all the necessary gestures and comments and was now leading them along the corridors of A Deck to their designated quarters, with due apologies for the lack of comforts.

Before meeting the Ululations, Tongue had hastily showered and changed clothes. Upon returning to his bedroom, he had discovered an ampoule containing a clear liquid. The accompanying instructions directed him to expose the liquid within a confined space. The effects, said the note, would take around thirty seconds and would be quite fatal to any equine-based life in the vicinity. How and when Tongue did this was up to him but, the note cautioned, it must be done before the ship arrived at Blah-Blah.

This was what now occupied his mind and made him chew his lip. Not an attractive look, he knew, but Miasma had told him he would get another opportunity to assassinate the delegates and now here it was — delivered by what appeared to be another Miasma agent aboard Space Scrap 17.

And that was a worrying thought.

Why had Miasma not told him that they had another agent aboard Space Scrap 17? Were they having him watched? This was an unwanted and annoying complication.

He could make any number of excuses for failing to carry out his orders. But not if a third-party had him under surveillance. If someone was watching him, how was he going to make sure the Ululations arrived safely at the talks? Did Miasma already suspect him of being a double agent?

Rounding a corner in the corridor, his mind elsewhere, Tongue almost walked straight into Jones coming in the opposite direction.

"Tongue!" said Jones.

"Jones!" said Tongue.

"Zebras?" said Jones, indicating the three Ululations.

Oh no, thought Tongue. This he did not have time for. "Ah. Yes, XO, allow me to introduce the diplomatic delegation from —"

"What . . . is the meaning of this?!" said Aching-Chestnuts, pointing a trembling hoof at Jones.

Tongue followed the indicated direction. Oh flaps.

"Ambassador," said Tongue, "Really this is a slight misunderstanding, you see —"

"Oh, what this?" Jones looked down at the logo proudly displayed on his T-shirt. A logo depicting a cartoon fist punching a cartoon zebra in the face. "Yes, I know what you're going to say."

"Jones, shut up and leave this to me," said Tongue, raising his hands in a placating gesture.

"You dare!" shouted PrancingHoof.

"You're right. It's a very sweaty T-shirt. But there's nothing wrong with that. I've been very sweaty of late."

"'Make yourself happy'," read AchingChestnuts, "'punch a zebra in the face'?"

"What that? Yes, it does say that. Which is fitting really because I bloody hate zebras. Really piss me off. And here you are, three lovely zebras who just happen to turn up from nowhere. Is that you Steve? Is this a joke? Who put you up to it? Was it Daisy? Come on, take off those stupid masks!" Jones stood with his fists balled, a manic glint in his eyes.

"XO, this isn't Steve," said Tongue, "these are —"

"Not a good time for a joke Steve! Here I am . . . sweaty . . . suffering the aftereffects of an ill-advised stim prescribed by that lunatic doctor! And you . . . you take advantage? Et tu Steve? Well, let me tell you these stims carry side effects of excessive urination and violent mood swings. And," he said, a sharp grin on his face, "I'm all out of excessive urination."

#

"You see, our discharge orifices were damaged

during the battle with the alien weapon," Daisy addressed the three Ululations on the bridge view screen.

"Ah," said NickersGaily, "One moment please Captain, I am receiving an urgent communication."

"Is it about the biscuits? Are the celebration biscuits ready?" asked the third Zebroid.

"Silence ButteryFetlocks, do you wish to spoil the surprise?" admonished StrangeGallop.

"Surely they will have baked delicious celebration biscuits of their own?"

"This is not their way."

"Oh," said ButteryFetlocks, squinting at the camera suspiciously, "weird."

"Silence both, we must commune!" said Nickers-Gaily, "Bring the Communing Biscuits!"

"Actually Captain," interjected Mic while the Ululations alternately communed and ate biscuits, "the discharge orifices were damaged when —"

"Shut up Mic," said Daisy. She kept her eyes fixed on the screen, reassuring smile in place.

"— you forced the XO to manually dock —"

"Mic, shut up," cracks began to appear at the corners of her strained smile.

"The Captain has perhaps forgotten the catastrophic consequences that resulted when she ordered the XO to manually dock the cargo pod and —"

Daisy's smile gave up and collapsed. She rounded on the communications officer. "Mic Vol, I am in the middle of a delicate first contact situation —"

"Um, Captain?"

"Not now Steve! While trying to prevent polluting the most sacred —"

"Captain Daryl"

The Ululations had completed whatever they had been doing and now regarded her sternly from the view screen. There was something very unnerving about being stared at by three zebras.

"Ah, yes, my apologies, I was just discussing some urgent matters with my bridge crew."

"Captain," said NickersGaily, "We have received some troubling news. Apparently one of your crew has violently attacked our diplomats."

Oh flaps, what now? "I'm sure there's some mistake, none of my crew would dare —"

"Captain," said Steve quietly.

"What is it?" hissed Daisy.

"Well firstly, Tongue reports that Jones —"

Daisy's shoulders dropped at the mention of Jones's name. "What's he . . . he hasn't . . . Oh flaps.

Zebras." Daisy pinched the bridge of her nose. "Nick-ersGaily, please understand, my XO has been under extreme pressure and has reacted badly to medication prescribed by our doctor, but I assure you —"

"And now," interjected NickersGaily, "your ship is discharging a large quantity of raw sewage onto our most holy grazing grounds. This is most peculiar. Can you explain before we completely destroy you?"

Daisy looked helplessly at Steve. "Yes," he said, "that was the other thing." An alert sounded on his console. Steve checked his board, his body suddenly tense and alert. He double checked the information displayed on the screens. "Orifices have stopped discharging sewage!"

"Oh, thank Jeebuzz!"

"Orifices have stopped discharging sewage . . . because they have completed discharging all one hundred and sixty eight million gallons of it. Onto the Ululation homeworld."

"Fuck."

On the main viewer ButteryFetlocks leaned toward the camera. "Herd leader," he said quietly, "shall I fetch the Revenge Biscuits?"

"THIS IS Shill Media [INSERT NUMBER OF HOURS IN YOUR LOCAL DAY CYCLE]. What's real? What's fake? Who cares? Stand by for a surprise statement by God Inc hosted by our regular political editor, Paxbot".

Sweat trickled down Sir Reginald's face as he squirmed beneath the studio lights. He nervously adjusted his eye-patch.

The Paxbot, adorned in a costume befitting a sex dungeon dominatrix, stared at him, rhythmically tapping a baseball bat on his open hand.

"You'd better make this fucking good," he growled.

"Ah, well, thank you for making the point, Paxbot because I think you will find what I have to say will be of great interest to you and your viewers."

"I doubt it. But carry on with your attempt to validate your existence, you piece of excrement."

"What I have to say concerns the nature of," Sir Reginald took a quick glance at a sweat stained handwritten note, "yes, the nature of our fundamental belief systems. As you know, God was proven to exist when an enterprising individual campaigned to remove the restriction preventing any company being named for a deity. Once removed, he immediately filed a company formation in the name of God Inc. And since, according to laws of the country formerly known as America, before the . . ." Sir Reginald made uncomfortable gestures indicating his preference not to go into the grotesque details, "the, you know, happened, American law stated that companies had the legal status of people and so he was able to legally prove that God exists."

"Get to the point."

"The point, ah, yes, the point, well the point is, the point is you see, the point . . ."

"You have no idea what you are talking about, do you?"

"Please not the face, we agreed, not the face!"

"Sir Reginald, have you actually read your brief?"

"Yes of course I have read my brief."

"Really, well it doesn't seem like you have any of the answers."

"Oh, I do," said Sir Reginald, daring to waggle a finger at Paxbot, "Oh yes I do. I am fully briefed in all the answers, just to an entirely different set of questions. Answers . . . well answers are overrated. Let me . . . let me ask you a question . . . frequently? What do you mean 'frequently'? Even more . . . even more let me ask you . . . because that is the very definition of democracy. I've not come here to answer a bunch of questions."

"Sir Reginald, why have you come here?"

"You see? Another question. You can't help yourself, can you?"

"Sir Reginald, do I take it from your drug-addled ramblings that you, and indeed the rest of the board of God Inc, are distancing yourselves from the proclamations of common decency uttered by God himself, Leroy Cakes?"

"Mr Cakes, I would remind you, is not God. Not until he is inaugurated as CEO and chairperson of God Inc. Until then his pronouncements may be considered questionable, debatable, proto-truths. Or to put it another way, total lies."

"So, his stance on 'innocent until proven guilty' even in the face of the ill-informed opinions of the self-appointed members of the Virtuous Council would be considered 'off message'?"

"Well, as I say, I am fully briefed with the answers, just not necessarily the answers to the questions you are asking. For example, how does this affect the cod quota? Hmm? Have you considered that? Go on, ask me something about cod quotas. Go on. I've got . . . I know loads about cod quotas . . . for some reason . . . seems I picked up the wrong brief . . . but yes, go on, ask me, I dare you."

"So, what will your stance be once Leroy Cakes is actually inaugurated?"

"Well let me tell you that there has been some very challenging science for cod stocks in the North Atlantic, and the cod have responded very well to implementation of the recommendations for conservation of cod stocks."

"By which you mean, they have gone extinct."

"Yes. Thus, bringing forward our conservation targets by several years."

"Sir Reginald, Archbishop of God Inc, thank you very much for sharing your last ill-informed words with us."

"Wait, what?"

The Paxbot swung its baseball bat which

connected, with a heavy 'thunk' sound, with Sir Reginald Ponce's head.

Execution complete, Paxbot turned to the camera with a reassuring smile.

"Next — in a dramatic turn of events, the Ululation government has agreed to join the Loose Association of Planets without the need for extensive talks and negotiation, thanks to some unusual circumstances involving a garbage recycling cargo ship. Lesley Bricks has the details — Lesley?"

". . . my fault, don't listen to him!" Jones awoke with a start. He looked around frantically, eyes wide, as if expecting multiple crises to jump out at him from every corner of the room wielding claw hammers and fangs.

Daisy lit a cigarette, sat back in her chair, crossed her legs and waited for him to stop gasping and jumping at everything in her cabin. He had done this three times before. Jerk awake, scream at things in her cabin like tables, corners of the room and the very concept of rooms, then collapse into unconsciousness for another twenty or thirty minutes.

To pass the time she absently read the health warning on the side of her cigarette packet: 'Interstellar Health Warning — Cigarettes can fatally improve your health'.

The cigarettes were just one of many inventions by an alien race called the Trope, who divided most of their time between having ideas, inventing things and travelling around the galaxy telling everyone they met how they had already invented anything and everything ever invented by anyone, anywhere. The Trope were mentally connected to each other via a level of reality they called the astral plane. But the astral plane was not exclusive to the Trope, as evidenced by hippies and 'woo-woo' folk everywhere pointing out that they knew about it too. As a result, any ideas any Trope ever had were instantly communicated not only to all other Tropes but also to anyone else who happened to be having a bit of a think at the same time. The Trope's only consolation was that the astral plane was an imperfect communicator. Even though everyone got the same general idea at the same time, much to the consternation of writers and artists everywhere, the ideas did not necessarily translate well.

One such idea was that of the cigarette. But where the Trope's invention concerned cigarettes made from highly addictive, health-promoting herbs, the idea as translated to other species completely failed to mention the 'health promoting' bit. Ultimately this didn't really matter as both versions of the cigarette turned out to be lethal, resulting in each packet of cigarettes requiring a health warning. In the case of Earth, because the cigarettes were addictive and toxic. In the case of the Trope, because they were addictive and healthy. Fatally healthy. The Trope became so amazingly fit that their redundant immune systems lost the ability to cope with even the weakest and least virulent of viruses of the alien races they visited. As a result of one such infection, the Trope prolapsed into extinction.

"Daisy," said Jones, suddenly sitting up on her couch. "I have questions. Why, how, who, what, when and if. And not necessarily in that order. I was on A Deck . . . oh Jeebuzz." Jones looked down at his blood-spattered clothing and knuckles. "Why am I covered in red paint? Was there red paint? The red paint trade show, yes, it's coming back now. We hosted a red paint trade show celebrating all the marvellous and wonderful shades of red paint it is possible to make. Did I give the keynote speech? Yes, I did, it's all coming back. 'Ladies and gentlemen thank you for coming here today to this wonderful convention. I think you'll agree it's been an excellent year for sales of red paint'. Was that what happened? Something like that? And then I got pissed and horrifically offended people and now I don't know what's happened or how much trouble I'm in. WHAT? TELL ME WHAT?"

Daisy handed Jones a cigarette and lit it for him.

She took a breath. "Well, shortly after Space Scrap 17 discharged our total cargo of sewage onto the most holy and sacred grasslands of the Ululation home world, you staggered onto the bridge covered in blood, said 'It's not —' and then collapsed unconscious. Tongue and Errol helped bring you down here to my cabin where you have been floating in and out of consciousness for the last three and a half hours."

"What about the convention?"

"No Jones, there was no convention."

"Are you sure? I've got a bloody good speech outline in my head. Why do I have a speech about fourth quarter predicted red paint sales in my head?"

"Probably a mix up on the astral plane. There was no convention."

"And the getting pissed and offending everyone bit?"

"Didn't happen. You have been suffering the somewhat spectacular side effects of the stim Doctor Smiert gave you."

"Oh good," he raised the cigarette to his mouth with a shaking hand. "So that's alright then."

"However, you did encounter the Ululation representatives on Deck A and proceed to attack them, shouting something about walking barcodes."

Jones's face dropped as fragments of memory began to string themselves together. "Zebras! There were zebras! On two legs. How were there zebras on two legs?"

"Zebroids is the term. Humanoid zebras. AKA the Ululation diplomatic delegation."

Jones looked at the blood spatters on his knuckles. "Oh flaps. Oh shit. I am in so much trouble. Wait, sewage? We discharged . . ." Jones's mouth continued to open and close but the only sound that come from it was a high-pitched squeak. He swallowed hard. "I suppose," he said quietly, rubbing a hand across his face, "I suppose they want to torture and kill us."

Daisy smiled. "Quite the reverse."

"They want to kill us and torture us? What kind of sick, twisted . . . no, wait I suppose it's better that way . . ."

"The High Herd of the Ululation government think you're a god."

Jones stared at Daisy blankly. "Sorry, no this stim, the words you're using are being substituted by nonsense. Say that again."

"Or, to be precise, they think you are the fabled

Herald of the Second Coming of their god, Gavin Starmane. And Space Scrap 17 is your mighty chariot and your coming was proclaimed by dumping raw sewage onto their world. And while they admit this is an odd way to make such a pronouncement, none of them are prepared to argue with you. Jones," Daisy sat forward, her face beaming, "they love us. They worship you. Literally."

"Why do they think . . .?"

"Apparently it was foretold that they would know the Herald by his repeatedly punching high ranking Ululations in the face while wearing the sacred garb."

"Sacred garb, what . . .?"

Daisy pointed at his blood-spattered T-shirt.

"Apparently your T-shirt contains an accurate depiction of Gavin Starmane. And the phrase 'make yourself happy, punch a zebra in the face' are the exact words contained in their holy text."

"You have got to be kidding me. That's . . . this isn't even my T-shirt."

Daisy spread her hands. "It's true. I've seen it. And because you, oh mighty Herald, have arrived, they think this is a sign they should join the Association and share their shielding technology with us, no questions asked. If war comes, they want to be on the side that heralds the second coming of their god."

Jones stood. "I've got to get rid of this T-shirt. I need to get to my cabin."

Daisy raised a hand. "I wouldn't. The Ululations are in there. They have decreed it a sacred space. They're waiting to cover you in unguents."

Jones raised his eyebrows, "Oh. Well, that doesn't sound too bad."

"Unguents they make from the spit of their high priests."

"Zebra spit?" Jones inclined his head, eyebrows knitted, considering. "No," he said eventually, "No. That sounds very unpleasant. Daisy I stink, I need a shower and a change of clothes."

"Don't worry," she said, standing. "Errol found your luggage, it's over there. You can use my shower."

"Thanks. I suppose you'll want to join me and worship me with a protracted celebratory body soaping?"

"No," said Daisy flatly. "Now bugger off. I need to talk to my Dad."

#

Tongue ran into his cabin and switched on the

news. His monitor filled with newsy graphics and urgent newsy music.

An urgent, newsy, dramatic voice announced, "This is Galactic News [INSERT NUMBER OF HOURS IN YOUR LOCAL DAY CYCLE]".

Cherry Pickings sat behind the news desk and addressed the camera with Concerned Face #7, the one reserved for news of great import. Concerned Face #7 usually indicated that something worth reporting had happened, and you were about to be told about that instead of the outright lies which made up most news output.

The music died down and Cherry began to speak. "We have just received reports that Leroy Cakes has died on the way to his inauguration as Aspirational Concept 36. His bodyguard, Razor Knuckleface, formerly Aspirational Concept 35, declined to comment due to the fact that he is also dead. Miasma Inc issued a press release three hours before the fatalities, stating that," here Cherry looked down at a DEVICE, "there are no indications of poisoning and they don't know anything about poison so even if there are indications of poisoning it is nothing to do with them or their recent acquisition of controlling shares in Poison Inc. Speaking with a Miasma spokesperson, our 'people who have suddenly died' correspondent, Lesley Bricks, pointed out that no one had actually raised the question of poisoning. We'll have more on this story later.

Coming up — tributes pour in after the sudden and mysterious death of our 'people who have suddenly died' correspondent Lesley Bricks."

Tongue switched off his monitor.

This was not good. Not good at all.

Although he didn't know it, Michigan Jones had rather neatly resolved Tongue's dilemma about his orders to assassinate the Ululations. Now, even if Miasma did suspect him of being a double, even if they were having him watched, no blame could be attributed to him. In any case, if they had suspected him, he was pretty sure he would be dead by now. No, his cover was safe, and the objective of the talks achieved. But the news of Leroy Cakes's murder was bad. Cakes, as Aspirational Concept 36, was to have prevented the onset of war by destroying first Miasma, and then God Inc. Now it seemed nothing could stand in Miasma's way.

Their last communication to him had been blunt — stay aboard Space Scrap 17 and await further instructions.

So. He was stuck here.

But for how long?

#

Daisy switched off her communications deck.

So, Daisy and Jones were stuck here now. Her father, the admiral, had been predictably ecstatic or 'effing chuffed', as he put it. Contracts and interview requests were pouring in. He had congratulated himself on his choice of executive officer. "You see Daisy, I said Michigan Jones would make an excellent EO. Bloody marvellous."

They were to stay in orbit around the Nonsense Sphere — the Ululations had promised to repair the ship for free — until the admiral sorted out their next contract.

"Looks like we're stuck with each other then," said Jones from the doorway to the bathroom.

Daisy turned from her monitor and gave Jones a long stare. She had originally intended to put him off ship the first chance she got. But now? Well, it hadn't been that bad, had it? And he had, after all, helped her through some tough times of late. She smiled. "So, it seems," she said. "I take it you have no intention of living with the Ululations?"

"Sod that, a planet full of zebras and being massaged with horse spit every day? No thank you," he scratched absently at the back of his neck. "No, I'd quite like to stay aboard if that's OK. I mean, I thought it was going to be a marmalade of nonsense at first but, you know . . . we sort of worked it out."

"We did. Just one thing though, something that's been puzzling me."

"Yes?"

"In the sick bay when I came in with the neural uploader. Smiert asked me what it was. You correctly identified it. But those things have been banned for decades. How did you know what it was?"

Jones shifted uneasily from foot to foot. "Well," he waved his hand airily, "I just sort of assumed, you know . . ." His voice trailed off.

"Huh. It's just that I hadn't explained my plan yet. So, you had no reason to assume anything."

"Oh no!" Jones dropped his towel and raised his arms, "I've dropped my towel, what a distraction!"

"How did you pass your XO exam?"

"You can see my cock and everything!"

Daisy blinked. "How did you pass your XO exam?"

Jones lowered his arms. "How? Brilliantly, of course. With aplomb. Or a plim, I forget which, does it matter?"

"You used an illegal brain patch as well."

"How dare you, you come in here with your, your accusations and you accuse me! Me, the Herald!"

"You did, though didn't you?"

"I did, yes."

Daisy shook her head. "Unbelievable."

"Alright, fine," Jones picked up his discarded towel, "we're both bad people. We deserve each other. So, what's our next mission?"

"Don't know yet," said Daisy. "But whatever it is, it can't be any worse than this one."

THE DENIZENS OF HYPOSPACE, entities who kept their real names a secret known only to themselves, regarded one another.

"Well then," said Boulder.

"Well then," said Filament.

"Our first round ends with a draw, yes?" said Boulder.

"It would seem so."

"Seem? Neither of us was able to land a killing stroke."

"It would appear so," agreed Filament.

"Well then."

"Appearances can be deceiving."

"Oh, I see," said the Boulder.

"What?"

"Nothing, nothing, carry on."

"No, what did you mean 'oh I see'?"

"Well, you're in one of your enigmatic moods again aren't you."

"Am I?"

"Stop it!"

"Fine," said Filament. "What did you think of Leroy Cakes?"

"I did not see him coming at all," admitted Boulder. If it had a finger it would have wagged it at its companion, "I had to alter my plans to deal with him."

"A mere feint — my real objective was to ensure the Ululations joined the Association."

"Pah! You think that will make any difference?"

"We shall see."

"I still think your choice of players is insane."

"There is much sanity in insanity."

"No there isn't."

The Filament paused for a moment. "No, you're right. I just couldn't think of anything enigmatic to say."

"That is the enigma of the enigmatic."

"Oh, that's good."

"Thanks."

"So then," said Filament, "Shall we commence with the next round?"

"After you."

"You are too kind."

"Too kind . . . or too cunnilingus?"

"Too . . .? Do you mean cunning?"

"Damnit yes," said Boulder. "Can I go again?"

"As you wish."

"Too kind . . . or too cunning?"

"We shall see," said Filament.

"Indeed, we shall," said Boulder.

"Yes, we shall," said Filament, unwilling to concede the last piece of enigma before the game recommenced.

"We shall indeed."

"I think we shall."

"Look just shut up and play," said Boulder, who suspected that this would go on for centuries if it did not intervene. It tensed, if boulders could be said to tense. "So, the next round begins."

"It began a long time ago."

"Oh, shut up."

The Filament made its move. It was, in Boulder's opinion, a very bad one.

<<<<>>>>

THE END

THE DOOMSDAY MACHINE IS DEAD

*BUT THE CREW OF SPACE SCRAP 17 SHALL
RETURN IN*

'1960s PURPLE SEX GAS'

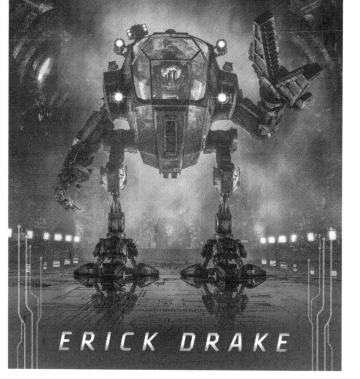

SpACE SCRaP 17

BOOK TWO

1960s
PURPLE
SEX GAS

ERICK DRAKE

"Huн."

On the bridge of garbage transport Space Scrap 17, second officer Steve Power inclined his head slightly. He checked the sensor readings once more.

"Huh," he grunted again.

Captain Daisy Daryl looked over at the helm station from her place in the captain's chair.

"Something troubling you, Mr Power?"

"There's some weird stuff going on outside the ship."

Daisy sighed and shut down the complex calculations she had been running from her command chair arm displays. In a way she was relieved to be turning her attention to something less complicated than ensuring her virtual farm had sufficient livestock to avoid being shut down by a virtual Miasma Inc.

"Mr Power, is that supposed to be an official report?"

"Nope."

"Would you like to make it an official report?"

"There's some weird stuff —"

"That is not an official report."

"OK"

Daisy tapped her finger on the arm of the chair. When it became obvious that no further comment would be forthcoming, she tried a pointedly loud 'Ahem'. Still nothing.

"Mr Power, what is happening?"

"I told you."

"Not officially."

"No, not officially, actually. Weird stuff. Outside."

Daisy sighed again. Clearly she needed to work on crew discipline. She just hadn't had time to properly work on anything since she had taken command. Not with having a vast, alien Doomsday Machine trying to turn them all into vast, alien Doomsday Machine dinner.

"OK Steve, tell me what's going on."

"Is that a formal command?"

"Second Officer, tell me what is going on outside my ship before I have you shoved into the waste recycling chute."

"We are surrounded by giant space babies. Oh," he said, glancing down at his monitors in surprise, "And our navigation weapons have opened fire on them."

"What? Why? How? But mostly why. And how. What?"

Steve's mouth opened and closed a couple of times as he groped for a form of words, or indeed, any words at all that could better describe what the sensor colonies on the ship's hull were showing him.

"Maybe I'm misinterpreting the sensor data," he said at last. "Oh, I know. I'll run a system check on my new face tattoos."

Daisy clenched her teeth. Not the bloody face tattoos again. No one had the heart to point out they made him look like a cross between a really angry Maori and a manic pagan priest.

"Nope," he said after a moment, "Green lights all the way. According to my face tattoos. On my face."

"Oh good," said Daisy noncommittally.

"Of course it is possible the sensors are just making shit up again."

"Making . . . Steve, are you going to start talking sense sometime soon?"

"Our sensors are basically vast colonies of specialist bacteria covering the hull. They haven't been upgraded since the ship was built and they get . . . well, bored. So sometimes, they just make shit up."

"Right."

"Well, that's why no one uses them anymore. They were declared horrifically unstable and withdrawn from the market. Most of the colonies retired and went into politics. Hang on." Steve activated the view screen.

"Ah. Well that's the what," he reported. "As to the why and the how, beats me."

Daisy rose from her command chair slowly. "Whu — ?" she pointed at the view screen.

Floating in space outside the hull of Space Scrap 17 were several . . . several . . .

"Giant space babies," Steve nodded his approval. "Good."

"Good?"

"Means the sensor colonies are still sane. Trust me, that's good."

"But where did they come from?"

"Us apparently. Ejected from cargo bay four. But that's not the interesting bit."

"It isn't?"

"No. That is." Steve pointed at the screen.

Daisy turned her attention back to the main view screen and watched as the space babies, gently bobbing around within foetal sacks in the silent vacuum of space, exploded as energy weapons tore into them.

"Steve, what's the source of those energy weapons?" Daisy span on her heel and headed back to the command chair.

"Also us," said Steve.

Daisy halted mid-step. "Computer, why are we shooting space embryos? Computer?"

"YES? WHO IS SPEAKING PLEASE?" Daisy winced as the distorted sound of the computer's voice interface bellowed across the bridge.

"Mic, can you do anything with that?"

Mic Vol, communications officer, considered the feasible options. Then he considered other, less feasible options, including half a dozen metaphysical ones. Yes, that one. He regarded the captain.

"No," he said.

Daisy gave him a flat look. "What about turning down the volume?"

"Ah." Mic rocked back, or rather his triangular

encounter suit did. "Might work," he conceded. He stabbed a button. "Volume decreased."

"Computer, you know who I am, you have voice recognition routines — use them."

"I COULD DO THAT, BUT IT WOULD INVOLVE ME RUNNING A REAL-TIME SEARCH AND COMPARE ROUTINE ON MY BINARY WAVE FILES, AND FRANKLY I HAVE WAAAAAAYYYYY TOO MUCH OTHER STUFF GOING ON RIGHT NOW. SO JUST TELL ME WHO YOU ARE."

Daisy and Steve exchanged glances. Steve shrugged.

"Computer has been a bit . . . stressy lately. Not surprising, the operating system is at release 0.01. Never had an upgrade."

"0.01?" Daisy cleared her throat. "0.01?" she said again, only this time in a voice less shrill and embarrassing. "Bloody hell, what level are they on now?"

"7.9.12.6"

"What about the regular upgrades?"

"You don't get regular upgrades with the free beta test version."

"Steve, we need to upgrade."

"We can't afford to upgrade."

Daisy massaged the bridge of her nose between her thumb and index finger.

"Alright. Fine. Computer, this is Captain Daisy Daryl. First, I want to know why we are shooting at giant space babies. Second, I want to know why there are giant space babies. Third, I want to know . . . what are giant space babies?"

"FIRST, WE AREN'T. SECOND, THERE AREN'T. THIRD, SUGGEST SCIENCE STATION REVIEW 20TH CENTURY DOCU-MENTARY 2001: A SPACE ODYSSEY."

"That will explain what they are?"

"WILL IT? GREAT — DO THAT THEN."

"Computer, we can see them. The sensor colonies can see them. We can all see them. Look for big, floaty exploding things outside the ship, and stop shooting them."

"Stop shooting who?"

Daisy froze.

"Is that any way to greet Daddy, little Miss Silly Knickers?"

Oh joy.

Daisy turned to the view screen, making sure to glare at everybody as she did so. One smirk, just one . . .

"Admiral, to what do we owe this honour?"

"So formal. She wasn't always like this of course."

"Dad . . ."

"No, she used to run around with her knickers on her head shouting 'look at me, I'm silly knickers'."

A shrill, staccato laugh escaped Daisy's lips. "Ah, the Admiral's famous sense of . . . bloody . . . humour. Dad, I'm in the middle of something, we need to do this later."

"So I heard. Why are you emitting giant space embryos? Have you run out of celebration fireworks? That's my girl, always able to improvise. The mark of a good captain."

"We don't know what they are. We're trying to find out and stop doing it. So, can we do this later? I need the view screen because the operating system is so out of date it contains trojan horses as old as the original trojan horse and we're reduced to looking out the window if we want to know what's going on."

"Captain," Steve actually raised his hand.

Daisy turned to Mic and drew her hand across her throat in a slicing motion, the universal sign for cutting communication.

Unfortunately, Mic Vol's race had a completely different universal sign for cutting communication.

So he just stared at her.

Daisy repeated the slicing motion, more urgent this time.

Mic Vol was puzzled. He turned 180 degrees to see if there was something behind him.

No.

He turned back.

Nonplussed, he mirrored the motion back at the captain.

"Jeebuzz, just cut the bloody channel!" Daisy shouted.

"Bit rude," muttered Mic. He pressed 'Mute'.

"Thank you," said Daisy, with all the restraint of a volcano overdue an eruption. "Steve, what is it?"

"Sudden idea. I can cross-link my face tattoos with the computer so it can see the floaty exploding things and stop shooting them."

Daisy opened her mouth to reply, then shut it again quickly. He had ordered the tattoos online one night after a heavy drinking session with Michigan Jones, the ship's XO. They had all seen the ads:

"Want to be more intelligent? Order our new bio-tek face tattoos. Don't like the idea? That's because you're stupid — which you won't be with our new bio-tek face tattoos! Worried about sentient bio-cultures in your face? Well, don't be — they'll grow on you. Literally! Order today."

The robo-tattooist had arrived the next morning while Steve was sleeping it off, and when he awoke — well, Daisy was certain they could have heard the screams on the Nonsense Sphere, the planet around which they were currently in orbit. Eventually he got used to the idea, just like the ad suggested, and now he wouldn't shut up about them. Ah, to hell with it.

"Face tattoos? Oh Steve, I hadn't noticed," she lied. "Are you sure they can do that?"

He shrugged. Good enough.

"OK Steve, do things 'n' stuff. Mic, re-open channel."

The admiral reappeared on the viewer. "About bloody time," he grumbled.

"Admiral, we really need to upgrade the computer. It's on the verge of collapse. You need to authorise the credits for us to buy a full working version of the operating system."

"I have an associate who can get a copy for me."

"No Dad, no under the counter software, no knock offs, rip offs or beta versions. We need a fully working, fully authentic version of ThingStuff. I'm sorry, but as captain of this ship I must insist. I need you to authorise the credits."

"Well, I'm sorry too silly knickers, but you can't have your pocket-money just now."

Daisy closed her eyes and took a deep, steadying breath.

Being captain was not working out the way she had imagined. Where were the rainbow unicorns and kittens? Where was her indomitable self-confidence? She had tried so hard to get the respect of the crew, she really didn't need this. What she needed was an efficient crew and the reassurance of a working computer that was slightly less neurotic than she was. Not that she was neurotic. Oh god, was she neurotic?

She headed for the back of the bridge.

"Mic, I'll take this in my broom cupboard."

"Ready room," said Steve.

"Ready room," she raised her thumbs in a gesture that resembled a flinch.

#

Daisy stood with her back to the door and waited while it slowly squealed itself shut. How long since the damn thing had seen a drop of oil? She would have fired the maintenance manager if they had one. Which they didn't, because they couldn't afford it. Damn it, she couldn't even fire anyone! She considered hiring a maintenance manager and then immediately firing them. The door finally closed, its fingernails-on-a-blackboard squeal falling silent at last.

She opened her private channel.

"Ah Daisy, there you are," the admiral grinned at her, his feet on his desk.

Daisy stifled a laugh. Free from the distractions of the bridge, she now noticed the highly noticeable. His new toupee had been styled in the most outrageous bouffant. She considered telling him how ridiculous it looked . . . he was her father after all. But no, she needed credits for the computer upgrade. Best to keep him sweet. For now.

"Father, you look . . . well."

"Father? Daisy, are you calling from the 19th century?"

"Well, our chief engineer is a Victorian industrialist."

"What?"

"Oh yes. Forget quantum mechanics, according to Mr Kettlewick the miracle of steam engineering is the future."

"What the hell are you babbling about child? Wait, are you in the broom cupboard?"

"It's my ready room. I wanted a ready room. This is my ready room. It *was* the broom cupboard. It is now my ready room. I gave all the brooms to Mr Kettlewick. He marvelled at the technology. Anyway, start again. Hello Dad."

The admiral looked confused for a moment. "We . . . we've already met Daisy. I saw you born!"

"Yes, I —" Daisy took a slow breath. "What can I do for you, Dad?"

"Ah, well I have news of your next mission. And even though you managed to dump a huge amount of sewage onto the Ululation home-world during your last mission, the Yerbootsian government have paid us three times the agreed price."

"Great, this ship seriously needs some upgrades."

"My thoughts exactly. And once we get paid for the next job, we can get them done."

"Good because we urgently need a — sorry, what? Next job? Why do we have to wait until after the next job? The Yerbootsians just paid three times our invoice total."

"Oh, you know about that."

"You just told me."

"Bugger. Well, yes they did. Unfortunately, I've already spent it."

"What? How? On what?"

"Do you like my new wig? It's bouffant. All the rage."

Daisy blinked at him. "Dad, the only thing holding this ship together is its own gravity. We just can't take on another mission with the ship in this state!"

"I'm sorry silly knickers, it's just . . ." His eyes grew moist. "You see, I've never actually had that many credits before, not even when I sold your sweet, fresh embryonic stem cells."

"You did what?"

"And I was walking past the Harrods designer wig section and they had this little beauty," he pointed to his head. "The money literally went to my head. I am going to be an absolute smash at this month's Wig Club. Peter Fondle will literally be sick. Now we'll see who's president for life. This is both the dog's bollocks and the bees knees of head wear. Imagine that!"

Daisy tried and failed.

"It's . . ." His eyes darted to the side as if he could no longer meet the gaze of the camera. He was silent for a moment, eyes moist once more. "It's the wig I've always wanted."

Her throat clenched, abashed by the sight of her father, this giant of a man, her guide and mentor, suddenly vulnerable. "Dad?"

Was that a tear on his cheek?

"Oh hang on, it's leaking again." He swiped at his cheek with a sleeve. "Oh, by the way, the High Herd of the Ululation government is concerned that their new prophet will not be staying with them on the Nonsense Sphere. I have agreed for them to send a biographer aboard. So they can document his profound utterances and so on."

Daisy stifled a grin. Michigan Jones would hate that. "That's great Dad, he'll love that. I'll tell him the good news personally."

"Good. Now Daisy, I don't think you're going to like this next mission but it's an errand of great mercy." His face grew stern and sombre. "Sometimes people can slip through the system, where there is no help. These people have a great need but no way to help themselves. Such times, such needs, require heroes to step forward."

Daisy was confused. "You want me to see if I can find some heroes?"

"No Daisy, you and me and young Michigan Jones are the heroes."

"Wait, what? No, we're not." She did not like where this was going. Their recent encounter with the Doomsday Machine had almost finished them. They were lucky to have got out in one piece. Because of that, and the minor fact that she was totally unqualified, she had had no time to properly learn the ropes of her new job.

"Well, you will be after this. A fatal epidemic of Plagues Disease has broken out on a planet called New Amsterdam. New Amsterdam is, how shall I say, a recreational world. A pleasure planet."

"Great. I'll organise shore leave," she said, flatly. "Been ages since I had a fatal epidemic. Had a recreational colonoscopy once."

The admiral nodded enthusiastically, "Me too."

"What is . . ." Daisy paused, her father's last comment sinking in. She shook her head, banishing the associated images. "What is Plagues Disease?"

"Nasty. Laboratory grown. The scientists over at Miasma were trying to find a health virus. One that promotes health and vitality and could be spread just like an ordinary cold."

"And?"

"They created the virus alright but it cannot distinguish between good and bad microorganisms. It kills all bacteria — including those necessary for healthy life. Now, there is a cure, but it cannot officially be made in sufficient quantities."

"Why?"

"It requires a vital ingredient to act as a catalyst. Bromidium."

"Ah," Daisy nodded. "Bromidium, yes, I see the problem."

"You've heard of it?"

"No."

"Well, it's incredibly useful but bloody difficult to make. The problem is, it's composed of three panacea atoms and one placebo atom. Technically, you can use anything for the placebo atom, you just believe that it *is* a placebo atom and hey presto, it is. But panacea atoms are trickier to produce. For those, you need the sheer, raw, naked, lubed-up power of an engineered supernova. And a very fine net."

"I don't see how we can help," said Daisy, "Unless the mission is to heroically stay the hell away from New Amsterdam, in which case sign me up."

"I said it cannot 'officially' be made in sufficient quantities. There is an alternative that behaves enough like Bromidium to be an effective cure for Plagues Disease. But it has to be distilled from a rare gas."

"Rare gas? What rare gas?"

"It's known as '1960s Purple Sex Gas'. PSG for short."

What new madness was this? "1960s Purple Sex Gas. Right. And just what is 1960s — what is PSG?"

"Ah, well, it's a fascinating story. Back on Earth

in the twentieth century there were many television entertainment programmes made in a period known as 'the spy boom'. Inevitably at some point in each episode, the secret agent hero would be knocked out by a gas fed into a locked room through an air vent. To make the threat of the gas visible to the viewer, the producers would opt for an industry standard purple vapour."

"Doesn't sound like it would have any medical applications?"

"Not then, no. But the purple gas manufacturers thought demand would last forever. They produced enormous quantities of the stuff. But eventually the popularity of the 'spy boom' went the way of the Western."

"The what?"

"The — oh, never mind. Suffice to say that demand for the purple gas dropped to zero. The manufacturers didn't know what to do with it, and so eventually they just loaded the surplus into containers and buried it. And that is where things would have ended, but over the centuries the gas mutated. It evolved a range of unfortunate properties. In small doses it acts as an extremely powerful aphrodisiac."

"I would have thought that would make it quite popular."

"And in larger doses it causes horrific and unpredictable mutations."

"Instead of acting as an aphrodisiac?"

"In addition to acting as an aphrodisiac. The results can be something of a nightmare, as you can imagine."

"So why do we have to get involved?"

"Well, as I say, in its raw state, PSG doesn't mix well with . . . well, with anything living. But when distilled correctly, it has the same effects as Bromidium. It can be used as the catalyst required to manufacture the cure for Plagues Disease. In quantity. Unfortunately, PSG is a banned substance across the galaxy. If caught smuggling, sorry, transporting it, the penalty is either a suspended sentence of community service or death by torture, depending on the judge."

"Forget it."

"Too late, the contracts are signed. There is a quantity of PSG en-route to you as we speak."

"What sort of quantity?"

"Vast."

"No. No chance. Even if I were stupid enough to break the law and risk the lives of my crew, this ship is a disaster just waiting to explode or implode or something else bad ending in 'plode'. There is no way we can undertake a dangerous mission like that with this ship. I wouldn't trust the computer to boil an egg."

The admiral pursed his lips. "Daisy, if we break this contract then we won't get paid and no one will work with us again. No credits, no upgrades."

"Forget it Dad, you can't blackmail me."

"No, fair enough. I blame myself really. I pushed you too hard. You're clearly not cut out to be captain. It's not your fault. I'll give Michigan Jones a call —"

"Go ahead. You really think I'm that easy to manipulate, that I'm that insecure, that I'd go to any extreme to prove myself to you or anyone else?"

"Yes."

He had her there. "Right, yes, but . . . well, he'll tell you the same thing. Even he's not that stupid."

"Are you sure?"

"No, you're right, he is that stupid. Alright, fine, I'm in. When does it arrive?" she said, instantly hating herself.

"That's my silly knickers. Should be with you in three hours."

"That's Captain, Admiral. Captain Daisy Daryl. If you're asking me to do this, you could at least show me some respect."

"You see, Michigan Jones wouldn't say things like that. He simply wouldn't care."

"Well, Admiral, Michigan Jones isn't the bloody captain. I am. Now if you'll excuse me, I have three hours to try to patch up my computer system and prep my crew for certain death."

"Oh, also," the admiral added, "I have arranged for a consignment of smart wigs to be sent to the ship."

"Smart wigs?"

"Three hundred and sixty-five of them. One for each day of the year. My collection will be the envy of Wig Club. Make sure they are forwarded to me upon completion of the mission."

"Yeah, sure, no problem," said Daisy airily, feeling anything but 'yeah, sure, no problem'.

The admiral beamed. "Ah, you are so my father's daughter."

"Wut?"

"You are so your father's daughter."

"You are my father."

"You are so my daughter. Bon Voyage Captain Daryl."

Daisy finished the call with a sigh and left the broom cupboard.

Now, where the hell was Jones? They had

three hours to prepare the crew for the arrival of vast quantities of the highly dangerous and massively illegal toxin known as 1960s Purple Sex Gas.

#

Daisy strode onto the bridge at a pace, the very picture of brisk efficiency.

"Ah, Captain," Mic said, "Cargo bay master reports we have taken on board a consignment of," Mic inclined his encounter suit's head segment, "'Smart wigs'?"

Daisy nodded, "Thanks Mic. Notify the admiral, would you? We'll have to deliver them after our next mission."

"Very well. Also our standard resupply requisitions have been delivered. Everything we asked for but there's a few substitutions. You will need to approve."

Typical, thought Daisy. She was such a useless captain even her shopping orders were countermanded. The admiral may have a point after all. She sighed. "Yes, fine. What are the substitutions?"

"We ordered semi-skimmed milk, for which they've substituted a crate of coconuts."

"OK, I suppose that makes sense. Sort of. Anything else?"

"Loaf of medium sliced bread for which they've substituted . . . a spanner."

"That makes less sense."

"New set of kitchen knives for the galley, for which they've substituted a 'slow, bitter relationship breakdown'. A six kilogram packet of cocaine —"

"Who the hell ordered cocaine?"

"No, that was the substitution. They're out of sugar. Instead of yoghurt, we have one hundred and seventeen packets of 'Itch-away Thrush Treatment'. Soy sauce has been substituted with a 'coy glance from the delivery driver'. No potatoes, so they've given us apples and instead of apples they've substituted potatoes. And finally, a crate of cock-rings instead of — oh, no, sorry, we actually ordered those."

"Who — no, I don't want to know. OK, approved. Anything else?"

"Oh yes. No recycling bags, so they've given us a consignment of 'Lucky Weapons'."

"Lucky weapons? What the hell are lucky weapons?"

"Ooh," piped in Steve, "Didn't think they were still around."

"What are they?"

"You know, things like 'lucky torpedoes" or 'lucky grenades' and the like. No need to aim, you literally just fire and forget because you'll always get lucky and hit the target."

"Sounds great, why have I never heard of them?"

"Outlawed. By digital marketing agencies."

"Why?"

"Well, they're the only product on the market that doesn't actually need marketing. By definition you'll always get lucky and have one when you need it. Marketing agencies couldn't have that, bad precedent, cuts them right out of the loop. They had them banned."

"Right, OK, Mic substitutions approved. Now, Steve, how goes the sensor recalibration?"

"Well the computer can now see the space embryos."

"Great, so it's stopped shooting them?"

Steve shrugged. "In a sense."

"In what sense?"

"In the sense that it isn't now shooting at them but only because it wasn't shooting at them in the first place."

"Well something was, are you sure that — no, never mind, we'll deal with that later. Steve," she lowered her voice, "I have a job for your face tattoos."

Daisy looked around conspiratorially. Steve, uncertain of what was coming, followed suit. She angled herself towards him. Confused, and now slightly alarmed, he angled himself away from her.

"Steve, could you hack the ThingsnStuff home omni-site? Specifically, the upgrade section?"

"Er, well yes, I suppose. To do what?"

"I want to upgrade the computer. We've got a vitally important mission coming up and I need the computer operating at full capacity."

He puffed out his cheeks. "Well, that would be a new experience."

"But I can't pay for it."

"Captain, I'm a navigation officer, not a thief."

"No, no, no, not thieving Steve. Borrowing. Look we need the computer to complete our next mission and we need to complete our next mission so that we'll have the money to buy the upgrade. See?"

A slow smile spread across Steve's face. He nodded. "Well, it's been a while. I'll see what I can do."

"Great." Daisy straightened, paused and looked around again. "Steve, can we do the thing?"

He sighed. Every captain he'd ever met . . .

"Fine."

Daisy beamed. "How long will it take Second Officer?" she said, loud enough for the rest of the bridge to hear.

"Two hours, Captain," replied Steve, equally loud.

"You've got thirty minutes."

"Oh no," Steve deadpanned, "Well, I'll have to bypass the . . ." Steve looked around then gestured vaguely at something across the room, "That thing over there."

"Excellent. Make it happen, Mr Power." Daisy turned and made to walk away.

"Captain?" Steve's voice stopped her in her tracks.

"Mr Power?"

He looked uncomfortable, "You . . . you know it'll really take a couple of hours, yeah?" he said, sotto voce.

Daisy looked around once more to make sure no one could have overheard. She turned back to Steve, gave a quick nod and marched away, pleased with herself.

How's that for initiative? She imagined explaining her brilliant command decisions to an interviewer at the Captain of the Year Awards. "How did I save millions of lives with a neurotic computer and undisciplined crew?" She'd probably add a knowing laugh. "Initiative. Courage. Innovation. Leadership." A better quote occurred to her, "To lead a ship, you need leader-ship." Interviewer looks impressed, audience claps spontaneously. She smiles and nods modestly.

Now to break the news to Michigan Jones. Somehow, she didn't expect spontaneous applause from him. Although he just might spontaneously combust.

ACKNOWLEDGEMENTS

Huge thanks to Samantha who puts up with my typing away in the wee, small hours and is very kind and forgiving of my first drafts. She provides endless encouragement and coffee. Thanks to editors Anya and Mark for making sense of my nonsense and to James for making it look good. Thanks to Rupert, the other half of the Space Scrap 17 creative development team, who must accept partial responsibility for creating the nonsense that would eventually coalesce into . . . whatever this is.

You're all spiffing.

ALSO BY ERICK DRAKE

Space Scrap 17

Book 1: *The Doomsday Machine*

The next book in this series is;

1960s Purple Sex Gas

For more information about Erick Drake content and books visit;

www.erickdrake.com

If you liked *The Doomsday Machine,* please leave a review on Amazon or Goodreads and help other readers like you find stories they'll like. Your reviews also tell the author what you like, so he can write more of it.

ABOUT THE AUTHOR

Independent author Erick Drake was an avid reader from an early age and the day his father brought home a computer, Erick knew he wanted to be a writer. "I'll never forget the moment I first saw that computer. It was pretty basic, just a glorified word processor really. But I felt anything was possible, I could go anywhere, do anything! Dad may as well have brought a TARDIS into the house. I started writing that day and have never stopped since."

He has written sketches for BBC radio comedy and in 2004 was commissioned by BBC South to write a Doctor Who TV story ('*The Paradox Device*' – production was cancelled due to some upstart genius called Russell T. Davies rebooting the series).

A career in IT meant that Erick was well placed to take advantage of the advances in technology that allow independent creatives to produce and publish their work. "I love the freedom that gives. My creative choices are my own. I can make what excites me and if the audience likes it too, well then that makes the slog worth it. Being an independent author is a bit like being a pirate or a Viking. Except without the violence and pillage. And the beards. And the ships. Actually, it's nothing like being a pirate or a Viking."

A life-long lover of science fiction, Erick lists among his favourites *Dr Who, Star Trek, Babylon 5,* Isaac Asimov, Robert A. Heinlein, Peter F. Hamilton, and James S. A. Corey.

Despite his love of fantasy and science fiction, Erick's natural inclination is to write comedy; "It was the first thing I wrote that I felt entirely comfortable with and which seemed to chime with the audience." Indeed, his comedy drama stage play '*Robin Hood – The Spirit of Sherwood*', was very well received as it toured east England. When the world gets too depressing, his go-to comedy is Douglas Adams' *Hitchhiker's Guide* series, Gary Larson's *Far Side*, *Dilbert* by Scott Adams, TV's *Blackadder, A Bit of Fry and Laurie* and sketch show *Big Train*. His audio collection includes his evergreen favourites, *Bleak Expectations* by Mark Evans and John Finnemore's *Souvenir Programme*.

But it is the draw of the oblique and the odd that informs most of Erick's absurdist writing within the realms of comedy, science fiction, fantasy and magical realism.

Currently living in Essex with his wife and cat, Erick is surrounded by the rich landscapes of the Essex countryside. His first full novel was the science fiction space opera parody '*The Doomsday Machine*', which was the result of a fever dream and too much cheese.

facebook.com/erickdrake616
twitter.com/@SpaceScrap17
instagram.com/erickdrake616

Until next time . . .

www.erickdrake.com

Printed in Great Britain
by Amazon